Ballroom Belles

Jean Morley

Ballroom Belles

MEMOIRS

Cirencester

Novels by Jean Morley:

Black Pearls

Talley Girl

Cotton Candy

Walking the Imp's Path

Intrigue and Elegance

The Reluctant Squire

House of Dreams

Published by Memoirs

MEMOIRS
PUBLISHING

25 Market Place, Cirencester, Gloucestershire, GL7 2NX
info@memoirsbooks.co.uk www.memoirspublishing.com

Ballroom Belles

ISBN: 978-1-909544-49-9

CHAPTER ONE

LADY AURELIA WINSLEY'S ballroom was only small when compared to those of the most grandiose houses in London, but this evening, as usual, she was giving the first dance of the season. It was February and although the season proper had not begun, this ball was given primarily for those young ladies who were just 'out'. It was the beginning of the rounds of balls and other entertainments they would face during the next few months when they hoped, not only to enjoy themselves, but to meet their future husbands.

The ballroom was decorated beautifully. The dark wooden floor was highly polished, and the large gold edged mirrors on the wall, with candles ensconced either side, shone brightly so that those assembled could see themselves and each other reflected to infinity. Where there were no mirrors, the walls were tastefully draped in pink silk, with arrangements of pink and white flowers set on marble pillars. The chandeliers, suspended from the ornate ceiling, sparkled and shone, the result of the hard work of the minions below stairs. There were gilt edged chairs arranged so that mamas and duennas could sit and watch the dancing, and keep an eye on their charges.

At the end of the room, there was a raised platform for the gentlemen of the stringed orchestra, who sat looking smart in black relieved only by white cravats and white wigs which were tied back with large black bows. They were now tuning up and sorting out their repertoire of music for the country dances and minuets that were to be played.

At the opposite end of the room was an alcove, comfortably upholstered in pink and which was reserved, as usual, for two particular ladies, Miss Euphemia Kelloe and Miss Drusilla Sonning. They were friends and well known to many. Lady Winsley knew they particularly enjoyed watching the first dances of the season, to assess the young ladies who they thought showed special promise. They knew the business and 'goings on' of most of the well to do, and although they were gossips, there wasn't an ounce of uncharitable thoughts in their bodies. If you needed to know anything about a certain well known person, they could tell you all about them without any trouble. They lived near to each other, their houses being in a desirable London district, clean but considered small in comparison with others. They were well looked after by a minimum of staff and the ladies communicated by maid if they wished to meet or had a particular piece of news to impart. To each other they were known as Effie and Dru.

Now sitting together, they looked like two large, plump cushions. They wore wigs, both of which were high standing and white, Effie's decorated with sparkling jewels, Dru's with pink rosebuds. Below, their raddled cheeks were powdered and patched and their fashionable rosebud lips looked odd on such heavily jowled faces. Large earrings dangled from their ear lobes, weighing them down. Their dresses, cut low across their ample bosoms, were of figured brocade, one in deep blue, the other in puce. They carried large fans, which sent out certain messages to anyone happening to be looking at them, but they primarily talked to each other privately behind them. Their pointed high heeled shoes were intolerably uncomfortable on their swollen feet but as they only tottered into and out of the ballroom, apart from going down to supper, of course, this didn't worry them overmuch, as they discarded them while sitting.

The orchestra began to play softly as guests arrived and Effie and Dru were alert and ready for their evening.

'Where is Sir Peter?' asked Dru. 'He usually stands with his wife to welcome the guests.'

'I can't see—oh yes, there he is,' said Effie. 'I expect he's been chatting to someone. He will absent himself when the dancing begins and return now and again to check if everything and everyone is all right.'

'You can't blame him,' said Dru. 'It's not an older man's idea of a pleasant evening, but he does support his wife, which is nice. She is very lucky.'

'Who is that, dear?' said Effie, pointing with her fan.

'Who are you looking at? Oh, I see, the plump girl with her mama. I don't know. Oh, now I remember, though, isn't it one of the Mullen girls? The poor woman has five daughters to bring out, hasn't she? What an expense that will be! Now who is that who has just come in behind her and is speaking to Lady Winsley?'

3

'I can't see,' said Effie, craning her neck. 'Oh dear, yes, I see who you mean, the girl with the flowers on her dress and in her hair and with necklaces and earrings and bracelets. I don't know her. Good gracious, she looks as though she has emptied her jewellery box over herself. Her mother should know better than to let her make such a spectacle of herself, but then, the mother is rather over decorated too, isn't she? She nearly puts Lady Winsley's chandeliers to shame.'

'Now, now, Effie,' said Dru, tapping her on her hand with her fan, 'that's not nice, dear.'

Effie giggled. 'Look,' she said, 'some young men have arrived. Quite a pleasant group. All friends, I should say. They will support each other. Let's hope they can dance.' She smiled. 'There will be some disappointed young ladies if they can't.'

'There are some very pretty gowns, Effie, aren't there? But that little fair haired girl shouldn't be in white. Her complexion is freckled and she would look better in yellow.'

'Oh, I don't know,' said Effie. 'Her hair is pretty.'

'Now who is that tall girl who has entered?' asked Dru.

'I think she's one of the Marlow girls. Yes, yes, there is her mama. The girl takes after her papa. He is tall and willowy. She'll have difficulty finding a husband,' said Effie, 'unless there's a gentleman who likes lanky lasses. But I will give her her due, she's dressed beautifully in that blue silk and she is pretty.'

'Just look at that group of girls,' laughed Dru, 'they're chatting, simpering and coquetting behind their fans, the

4

naughty pusses. Let's see how many beaux they catch that way.'

'More young men have arrived, that's good,' observed Effie, 'all beautifully dressed too. They mean business...'

'Or,' Dru interrupted, 'their papas have seen them turned out properly beforehand. It always makes me laugh. They come in small groups to give each other support, I suppose.'

'Yes,' said Effie, 'but I don't blame them. I mean the young ladies have their mamas or someone with them, don't they?'

'I like to see the men's fashions, too,' went on Dru. 'That dark boy looks wonderful in maroon with a cream waistcoat, and plenty of lace at neck and wrists, and that fair young man in peach looks good enough to eat.'

'Look,' said Effie, 'who is that pretty girl? Is that her mama with her, do you think? She's dressed very sweetly in pale pink and white, isn't she? She has little flowers down the front edge of her skirt, rosebuds, I think, and in her hair to match, too. Now, look at that. She has gone and sat with that lonely girl over there. How kind. Perhaps she knows her, though.'

'I don't think so,' said Dru, 'her mama has introduced herself to the older lady there.'

The two onlookers stared and smiled at this kindness while the orchestra struck up for the first country dance. Partners were found and the evening began.

Lady Winsley, relieved from her post of welcoming her guests, began to circulate to have words with friends. As she passed Effie and Dru she smiled at them. 'Are you all right, my dears? Shall I send you some champagne?'

'How kind,' said Effie, 'but first may we congratulate you on your ballroom and invitations to all these young people. Don't they all look lovely, like butterflies, a myriad of colour!'

'Could I ask, dear Lady Winsley, who is that pretty young lady in the pale pink dancing there with the dark young man?' asked Dru. 'She seems to know just how to go on.'

'Ah, she is Lavinia Meadows. Her mama is with her and they have just come from their stay in Bath. She very sensibly took her daughter there, so that she could learn how to go on at the dances, you know, where they are very strict. The elder daughter is now married and I believe there are two younger boys.'

'She will do well with her good looks and figure,' said Effie.

Lady Winsley nodded and said she must leave them for a while but she wouldn't forget the champagne.

'I'll tell you who isn't here tonight,' said Dru.

'Who is that, dear?'

'Why, the young man who's a beautiful dancer and handsome, too,' said Dru. 'I mean, compared to these clodpoles he would put them all to shame. Just look at that young man, I'm sure he has trodden on his poor partner's foot. She doesn't look too pleased, does she?'

'I don't blame her, but when you say a handsome, beautiful dancer, are you talking about Naughty Nick?' asked Effie.

'Oh, that's right. He's lovely to look at and to watch,' said Dru dreamily.

'But my dear,' admonished Effie, 'Lady Winsley wouldn't invite him amongst all these green girls, now, would she? Their mamas would soon take them back home again, you know.'

'Oh yes,' sighed Dru wistfully, 'but I wish I was younger.'

'Now you know that's rubbish. He's accomplished in all the niceties but he is not nice as you very well know,' said Effie severely.

'Look at those young men who have just appeared dressed in their regimentals. There is something about a bright uniform that makes them look so handsome, isn't there? See, that group of young ladies is already encouraging them with their nods and smiles,' said Dru.

'The hussies,' laughed Effie. 'I know what you are going to say next, that Naughty Nick would look wonderful in regimentals. If he was, all the girls would be disgraced and you know it, Dru.'

'Yes, I know, but he is so beautiful to watch,' said Dru with a sigh.

'So,' said Effie, eying the glasses of champagne that a servant had just brought for them, 'who are the favourites going to be to make a good marriage, do you think?'

For some time they watched and noted the behaviour, the looks and the dancing of all the young people present, discussing each one and making mental notes of who impressed them the most, until Lady Winsley whispered as she passed them: 'After the next dance, my dears, supper will be served, so if you wish to go before the rush...?'

'Thank you, dear Lady Winsley, we will go at once,' smiled Effie.

It took a little time for them to insert their plump feet into their dainty shoes but at last they were able to stand and totter out of the room as the last minuet was danced before the interval. Carefully they managed to descend the circular stairs to the floor below and entered the refreshment room to find their efforts rewarded with a display of small lobster patties and other tasty savouries, creams, ices and little cakes. They chose a variety of each plus more champagne and sat together in a corner where they could watch the entrance of the rest of the guests.

In due course the young people and their chaperones made their way down to supper, all chattering, laughing and eagerly asking for drinks of refreshing lemonade, or stronger ones for those who could take, or who were allowed, alcohol. Effie and Dru noticed the ones who were sensible and those who, through sheer bravado, drank unfamiliar liquor. They nudged each other. 'We must watch him,' they whispered, and sometimes they agreed to watch a certain 'her'. They themselves refreshed their palates with champagne in between the large variety of delicacies they had chosen.

Eventually, their appetites appeased, they decided they should make their way back, as it was decidedly warm where they were. Once more they carefully climbed the stairs and found their way back to their seats in the ballroom. Once there, they opened their reticules to bring out their face powder to repair the ravages to their faces caused by the heat and a little too much alcohol. When they thought they were respectable once more, and assuring each other (with hardly a glance) that they were looking delightful, they settled down for the next half of the evening, discussing the various young people who had made an impression on them and whom they would report as 'promising' to Lady Winsley.

The orchestra, having been provided with suitable drinks during the interval, was now tuning up ready for the second half of the evening. Lady Winsley had thoughtfully provided her guests with a light entertainment next in the form of professional dancers, to let her guests 'digest their suppers,' as she had said.

The ten dancers were from the theatre and danced prettily as Effie remarked. They held half hoops of roses, under which they moved in and out with coloured ribbons. It was all beautifully performed with grace and elegance. At the end of it all the male dancers threw handfuls of rose petals to the ladies in the audience while the girls gave a rose to a certain few of the gentlemen who jostled each other to receive the precious gift.

The dancers made their exit to partake of supper while the young ladies and gentlemen returned to dancing their minuets.

'Now,' said Dru, 'we shall have to decide who of the young people will be the ones to watch in the future. A few stand out as promising, don't they, Effie?'

Effie, red in the face from concentrating on kicking off her shoes once more, took a deep breath after this achievement and replied somewhat breathlessly. 'Yes, dear,' she puffed. 'Who have you thought of? Do you think the young man in peach?'

'Yes. Oh, oh, look!' exclaimed Dru, pointing with her

fan. 'Look, that dark boy has forgotten his steps. Now they're in a mess.'

The young people were dancing a country dance and the young man in question had really confused the order of the dance.

'Oh, dear,' said Effie with a grin, 'they *are* in a muddle. But they are sorting themselves out. Yes, look, everyone knows where they are, now.'

The dancing went on. 'You know,' said Dru, 'I had that young man in mind as promising but now I don't know.'

'He probably had a little too much to drink at supper,' nodded Effie wisely. 'But there are others we can point out.' They began the serious business of choosing.

It wasn't long after this before Lady Winsley came to them. 'Well, my dears, have you had an enjoyable evening?' she asked, with a smile.

'Oh, the best, dear Lady Winsley,' enthused Effie.

'It has been wonderful, as always,' endorsed Dru.

'So,' said Lady Winsley, 'tell me which young man you favour.'

'Well,' said Dru, confidentially, 'we liked the one in pink. He is a good dancer, and so also is the one in cream and gold.'

'But our favourite,' said Effie, 'is the fair boy in dark blue. He behaves as he should, seems friendly without pushiness and dances well.'

Lady Winsley smiled. 'I'm so pleased you chose him. He is my nephew, John, you know.'

Effie and Dru beamed at each other.

'Now, which of the young ladies did you choose?' asked Lady Winsley.

'We liked the plump little Mullen girl but our favourite, who we think will make a good marriage, is the fair haired girl who I believe you said was Lavinia someone or other,' said Dru.

'Lavinia Meadows,' said Lady Winsley.

'That's right. She behaves well, dances well, and has a certain something which stands out from the others,' finished Effie.

'Well, ladies, we shall see what happens, won't we?' said Lady Winsley. 'Now, would you like me to call for your carriages for you before everyone else? We shall be finishing after the next dance.'

'Thank you, dear Lady Winsley. It has been a most pleasant and enjoyable evening.'

Lady Winsley moved away while Effie and Dru heaved themselves up from their couch in the alcove, gathered their belongings together, and sailed forth to their respective carriages, Effie now carrying her shoes.

CHAPTER TWO

'**MAMA,** wasn't that the most enjoyable evening?' asked Lavinia Meadows as they travelled back in their carriage to their house in Mount Street with their feet on hot bricks as the night was so cold. 'Lady Winsley was so kind to invite us, wasn't she? And didn't the ballroom look splendid? And I could have eaten much more of the delicious food than I did, but I remembered you saying not to look greedy just in time. And I only drank lemonade as you bade me. And I danced every dance!' she finished with a sigh of satisfaction.

Her mother smiled tolerantly at her. 'Yes, Vinny, I agree with what you say. It was a lovely evening and everyone was very kind, but don't let your Papa hear you bragging, my love. You were very fortunate to be invited to dance every time. Not everyone was, you see.'

'No, Mama, of course I won't say anything to anyone else but I thought it would be between ourselves as you were there.'

'Then that is all right, dear,' said Mrs Meadows with a smile. She realised that her daughter was pretty and had a smile that won hearts, so she was careful not to let her think too much of herself. On the other hand, Vinny was very accomplished in most things she undertook, not like Anne, her elder daughter, but who had made a comfortable and happy marriage anyway. Mrs Meadows thought that Vinny would have no problems finding someone who wished to marry her. In fact, after a while it might be difficult keeping away prospective swains, but she was determined to see that her daughter behaved herself in every way possible so that when the right gentleman came along she would have nothing for which to reproach herself.

'Oh, Mama, I thought Rose and her mother were very nice and I said I hoped to meet Rose again. I hope you don't mind.'

Rose and her mama were those who were sitting alone at the ball until Lavinia and her mother arrived.

'Yes, of course, dear, if you wish. Her mama is a quiet and refined lady, I thought.'

'Rose is shy, you know, but really she is very pleasant. She was telling me she has a brother and I believe there are some younger children, too. I told her I had an elder married sister and two younger brothers. I don't think she lives very far away from us here in London.'

'Very well, Vinny, we will see about a meeting sometime. Now we are nearly home so can we have less chatting as we enter the house, otherwise you will wake up everyone? And don't keep Betty up any longer than you need.'

Lavinia and her mama were let into the house by a servant who gave them their candles, curtsied and said a tired 'Goodnight.'

'Thank you, Mama,' Lavinia whispered on the landing upstairs, as she kissed her mother goodnight before opening

13

her bedroom door. She found Betty, her young maid, waiting for her and trying to keep her eyes open.

'Oh, Miss, there you are. Was it a good evening?'

'Thank you, Betty, it was lovely, but I will tell you about it tomorrow. If you help me out of my dress and put away my jewellery, I can manage everything else. Go to bed, you have to be up early in the morning.'

'Thank you, Miss. I've placed a hot brick in your bed.'

'Do you have one in yours?'

'Oh, no, Miss.'

Lavinia dived into her bed, bringing out the wrapped hot brick. 'Here you are. My bed is lovely and warm so you take this and you will soon be asleep. I'm quite warm with all the dancing.'

'Thank you, Miss, and good night.'

It was a long time before Lavinia slept, as she went through the evening in her mind. She had enjoyed everything, it had been wonderful, but she had not met any young gentleman for whom she could care, or whom she even remembered. She pondered this, tucked under her bedclothes, and came to the conclusion that perhaps an older man was her destiny. She wrinkled her nose. She didn't like this idea and finally decided she had no need to worry at the moment, anyway. After all, this was only the beginning of the London season and there was still plenty of time to find a husband, but she was determined it would be someone she loved. Having satisfied herself with this decision she snuffed out her candle and cuddled down to sleep.

Mr Percy Meadows, Lavinia's father, had taken a house for the season in Mount Street, in the Mayfair area of London. He had done the same for his elder daughter, Anne, just over two years previously, and thought it only right to do the same for Lavinia. He wasn't a wealthy man; he referred to himself as 'comfortably off,' and one season would be all Lavinia would have. After all, he had two sons to provide for, too. Usually the Meadows family lived on the Kent border in a comfortable house, which stood in its own grounds. These weren't large, only boasting a small terraced garden, a medium sized lawn and a small woodland area beyond. However, this was a wonderful place to play robbers and highwaymen, and the boys had had much enjoyment there when small. Occasionally it had been known for their sister to join in the fun too. They were all happy there and were friendly with their neighbours and the villagers, and enjoyed life in general.

Mr Meadows was a pleasant faced man, not handsome, but his grey eyes were humorous and he was a kind father and a considerate husband. Now, as they sat down to breakfast the following morning, mindful of what was expected of him, he asked Lavinia if she had enjoyed herself the previous evening. She remembered her Mama's words and said merely that it all had been lovely and the ballroom was beautiful.

'What was the food like, Vinny?' asked stocky twelve-year-old John, tucking into his plate of various cold meats.

'Wonderful,' said his sister. 'I could have eaten much more than I did but as I wished to dance afterwards it

15

wouldn't have been a good idea.'

'Pooh,' said John, waving his forkful of beef, 'just like a girl. Food is much more important.'

'Yes, John,' said his father, 'but I don't need it brandished in my face.'

'Sorry, Papa,' said John, not looking a bit repentant.

Edward, his older brother by four years, was now becoming aware that he was his father's heir. Not only was he studying and hoping to gain a scholarship to Oxford, he was trying to learn the arts of fencing and dancing. Now he looked at John. 'Wait until you're older. You will have to learn to dance like I do. If you don't,' he continued, seeing the look of distaste on his brother's face, 'you won't be invited out and therefore you won't be able to partake of the suppers.'

'Ugh! I shall refuse to go, then, because I think I'd rather learn bare knuckle fighting. At least your opponent is at the end of your arm and not with a length of steel between you. It would be more fun, I'm sure if...'

'That will do. Did you not hear me, John?' said his father, loudly. 'Eat your breakfast in silence, please. I will not have brangling at the table or this kind of talk.'

After that all was quiet, until Mrs Meadows spoke to her husband. 'What are you doing today, dear?' she asked softly.

'Well, if these two are going to behave themselves, I thought perhaps they might like to visit a museum and have a look around some parts of London.'

'Yes, please, Papa, and could we go to the Tower?' asked John, hurriedly swallowing his mouthful of food and not a bit abashed by his father's previous words. 'And could we see the river Thames with all the boats? Perhaps we could go on the ferry. I know they take you over to the other side and we might see some floating bodies because my friend Josh at home said…'

'Quiet!' said his father in his loudest voice. 'I will not have this conversation at the table or at any other time. You will therefore be silent for the rest of the meal, John.'

'In that case, Lavinia,' said her Mama, ignoring her husband and son, 'shall we visit the shops a little later? I've a few small items to purchase and perhaps we could look at more material.'

'Yes, Mama. Would it be too chilly to walk in the park for a few moments, do you think? I know the flowers will not be out, but I should like to see a little of the park.'

'We will bear it in mind, Vinny.'

'In that case, my dear,' said Mr Meadows, 'you take the carriage.'

There was a chill wind blowing that morning and although Mr Meadows and his sons cared nothing for this, the boys even thinking it great fun to chase after hats that had been blown off heads, they soon found a hackney to take them to the heart of London. John laughed out loud, though, as an elderly gentleman, removing his hat to bow to a lady, found his wig lifted from his head in a strong gust of wind. Edward instantly clouted his brother but they both thought it funny and wondered how the gentleman would retrieve it as it finally deposited itself on top of the railings further down the street.

Meanwhile, Lavinia and her mama tied on their bonnets securely, hid their hands in muffs against the cold, and sallied forth to visit the shops. Lavinia was very pleased with her bonnet, a particularly fetching one of dark blue velvet, the colour of her eyes, and decorated with cream ribbons. Their carriage was chilly and Mrs Meadows wished she had ordered a hot brick for their feet to have been placed inside, but she told her daughter that they would soon warm themselves once they were walking or inside the shops. They were soon there and after telling the driver to return for them in two hours' time, they set off.

They thoroughly enjoyed themselves looking in the jeweller's window, pointing out a pretty bonnet in another and sighing over the beautiful gowns displayed in a very fashionable boutique. Then they came to a large emporium, which sold fabrics of all kinds, some quite cheaply. They went inside and looked carefully at the silks and lace. 'I think,' said Mrs Meadows, after casting an expert eye over all of them, 'this patterned blue silk would make up beautifully for you a new dress, Vinny. Would you like it, do you think? And with an underskirt of this frilled lace it would look sweet. We could edge it all with blue forget-me-nots, you know. And you could wear my necklace of sapphires. It is very delicate and just the thing for a young lady.'

Lavinia's eyes sparkled. 'Oh, Mama, thank you, and I have your white silk fan I can use, too. But who will make the dress?'

'I know of a dressmaker, or I did, called Madame Benét. Her establishment is not far from here. She made gowns for Anne, you know. I hope she is still there. Shall we visit her now and see if she can make it for us in time for Lady Brigham's ball? If she can, we will come back and purchase the material.'

'Is she a French lady, Mama?'

'No, dear. I think her real name is Bennet but it is fashionable to be thought French in the world of gowns. I believe it attracts more business.'

'Oh,' said Lavinia, thinking Madame's real name was preferable.

Fortunately, Madame Benét was still in the same small, elegant shop in the side street and she was delighted, she said, to make Mrs Meadows' daughter's dress. Mrs Meadows said they would go back and purchase the material, but Madame suggested her assistant should accompany her while she took her daughter's measurements and showed her some patterns.

It was some time later that Lavinia and her mother left the shop, pleased with their morning's achievements.

'We have time to take a quick look in the park, if you wish, Lavinia, before returning for lunch,' said Mrs Meadows.

'Oh, yes, please, if we walk briskly we shall keep warm. I'm told we may see some important people in their carriages and perhaps some will be riding. Would you know them, Mama, if we do?'

'I might, but as we don't move in the highest circles of society, perhaps not. But a little brisk walk will do us good.'

So they set off. The park was clean with some evergreen

bushes and beautifully shaped trees. Most of the people either were in enclosed carriages or were riding, and not many were walking in the cold wind. All of a sudden Lavinia spotted a group of people. 'Look, Mama, isn't that Rose and her mama with some friends?'

'I believe it is. Rose looks a little cold and unhappy. Perhaps you should speak to her, Vinny.'

They walked towards the group and when Rose saw who it was, she smiled and drew her mother's attention towards them. After that they were drawn into the group conversation, mainly about the previous evening. Lavinia couldn't help but notice that Rose looked pale and worried and while everyone else was talking Lavinia quietly asked her if anything was wrong or was she just very cold.

'Oh, Lavinia,' Rose said, 'yes there is indeed something wrong, but I cannot tell you here, Mama will be listening. But please, will you help me?'

'Well, I'll try,' said Lavinia, hoping she hadn't let herself into something she shouldn't have done.

'Could I come and visit you sometime today, do you think? You see, I must do something tomorrow or it will be too late.'

'Too late for what?' asked Lavinia, beginning to be intrigued.

'Could I come and visit you this afternoon, do you think? Then I could tell you all about it. And can you keep a secret even from your mama?'

'Yes, of course.' Lavinia was really interested by this time. 'Mama, excuse me, but could Rose come and visit this afternoon?'

'Yes, of course,' said Mrs Meadows. 'Would you care to come as well, Mrs Smythe? Come and take tea with us.'

'Why thank you, that is very kind,' said Rose's mother.

'Good, we will see you both later then and we can finish our conversation where it is warmer. We shall catch cold if we stay longer in this wind.'

Lavinia and her mama moved away from the group to find their carriage awaiting them. Both were pleased with their shopping and Lavinia wondered what it was that her new friend had to tell her that afternoon. She hoped it was something exciting.

CHAPTER THREE

MRS SMYTHE and Rose visited in Mount Street that afternoon as arranged, to be received by Lavinia and Mrs Meadows, who was dressed in an elegant afternoon gown of blue silk while her daughter looked charming in pink and cream. Mrs Smythe, wishing she had the looks and figure of her new friend, and Rose, the charm that so became Lavinia, was welcomed warmly into the house which was certainly an improvement on the biting wind outside. She and Rose were shown into the parlour where a large fire burned and were seated in comfortable chairs. Mrs Smythe, relaxed and smiling, said how pleasant it all was and how kind Mrs Meadows was to invite them.

'We are very pleased with this house,' said Mrs Meadows. 'But we were able to stay here before when we brought out my elder daughter, you know, so we knew how comfortable it was. She is married now so it was well worth it.'

Mrs Smythe said the house that they had taken wasn't quite so large and comfortable. Mrs Meadows also learnt that Mr Smythe was of a sickly nature and wasn't too happy away from home, but he was doing his best. She was also worried about her son. She felt he needed his father's guidance more and his companionship and so lulled by the warmth, and drinking the excellent tea provided, she went on and on, unburdening herself to a sympathetic listener and feeling much better for it.

Meanwhile, Lavinia and Rose sat together on a couch talking of the previous evening. Rose quietly murmured pleas to Lavinia to speak privately with her and so, after they had drunk their tea, Lavinia asked her mother if she would excuse herself and Rose as she wished to show her friend the necklace she would wear with her new dress. Permission was given so it was a relieved Rose who followed her new friend upstairs.

'There is a nice fire in my room too,' said Lavinia, 'so we shouldn't be cold.'

'How lucky you are,' said Rose as she entered the bedroom, and sitting down, stretched her fingers towards the fire to warm them.

'Now,' said Lavinia, 'what is your problem and how can I help?'

'Well,' said Rose, licking her lips as she smoothed her dress of crimson silk, 'it isn't my problem, exactly, it is my brother's. You see, he went out with some friends the other night and came home a little on the go, you know.'

'No,' said Lavinia with a puzzled frown, 'I don't.' Then as the light dawned she opened her eyes wide, saying: 'You don't mean he was drunk?'

Rose nodded. 'I'm afraid so and I think he and his friends became involved with others and something happened. I don't know what exactly, but the result is he has to meet this man and fight a duel.'

'Good gracious,' said Lavinia, 'what was it all about?'

'I don't know and Ferdy can't remember either. He was with his friends in this place and he became involved in an argument. I—I don't think it was a very nice place, he did mention some kind of women.'

'How old is your brother, Rose?'

'He's a year younger than I, but he is tall and looks older.'

'But,' said Lavinia, 'he is under age then. It is illegal to duel if you are under age.'

'Oh, dear,' said Rose, plaiting and unplaiting her fingers. 'That makes it all the worse, doesn't it?'

'Is he good at fencing?' asked Lavinia.

'N-no, I don't think so. He hasn't been taught, anyhow.'

'Well then,' said her friend knowingly, 'he cannot meet this man. What he must do is to find out where the other man lives and go round and apologise for whatever happened and tell him he is under age. Would his Papa go with him?' Lavinia thought if Edward had been so stupid, Papa would certainly accompany her brother.

But Rose was shaking her head. 'No,' she said. 'Papa must never know, neither must Mama. It would nearly *kill* them.'

Lavinia thought if Rose and her brother knew that such things would upset their parents, they should refrain from doing them. Aloud she said: 'Could you go with your brother, Rose? You would have to take a maid with you, of course.'

'Oh, no, no, I couldn't. I wouldn't know what to do or say.'

Lavinia thought this was rather a poor spirited answer.

'Well, what else can be done? What would happen if your brother just didn't arrive at the duelling place?'

'But I don't think that can happen as they have seconds, you know, who are responsible for arranging the meeting and seeing that their principal arrives on time.'

As Lavinia, chin in hand and a frown on her brow, pondered all this, footsteps sounded outside her room. She went to open the door. 'Is that you, Edward?' she called.

'Yes,' he answered as he opened his bedroom door.

'Could you come here a moment please?' called his sister.

'Just a minute and I'll be there.'

'That's Edward,' Lavinia explained to Rose. 'He's my eldest brother. He is sixteen but he might be able to suggest something we can do.'

After a few minutes Edward came in and was introduced to Rose. He gave her a slight bow and as Rose was preparing to get up to curtsey, Lavinia waved her to remain seated. 'Sit down, Edward, please and listen, as we have a problem.' Edward was told the story.

'What a stupid thing to do,' he commented when Lavinia had finished.

'Rose and I realise that,' said his sister, 'but it doesn't help, Edward.'

'If he goes and takes his father with him, the other man can't do anything about it if he's under age.'

Lavinia explained why neither of them could go, as his parents weren't to be told.

'Well, perhaps the friends he was with could...' began Edward.

'Do you think we should go, Edward? I mean Rose, you and I?'

'What, to a gentleman's residence?'

'I know it's not really the thing to do but if we took our maids with us and you escorted us...?' She left the sentence unfinished, looking hopefully at him.

'But where does this man live and who is he? Do you know, Rose?'

'Ferdy said he lives in Grosvenor Square but I don't remember his name or his number.'

'Not much help there,' said Edward, 'but Grosvenor Square isn't far away. It's a smart area so we could find out somehow, I expect. And whoever he is, he must have a large amount of money to live there, as it is an exclusive part of London. Therefore, I would imagine he is an older man, so surely he would understand. He probably has a wife, too, so I'm sure if they were told it was all a misunderstanding and apologies were given it would be all right.'

'Would you go with us, Edward? If you, Rose and I go with our maids, that would be acceptable, wouldn't it? And you could hire us a hackney, couldn't you?'

'Have you any money for one?' asked Edward.

'Well, I have a little,' said his sister.

'I expect I could get Ferdy to pay. After all, it is because of him we are going,' said Rose hopefully.

'We could walk. It's not far,' said Edward.

'But it's so cold,' complained Rose.

'The thing is,' said Lavinia, 'are we going to visit this man or not?'

'We must,' said Rose, now wringing her hands. 'If Papa learns of Ferdy mixing with such people he will be ill and Mama upset.'

'Edward?' asked Lavinia.

'Oh, all right. I'll accompany you but that's as far as I'll go.'

'Thank you,' said his sister. 'And will you face this man, Rose, and tell him your brother is under age?'

'Oh dear, I know I should but—but could you do that, Lavinia? You are so—so capable.'

'But Rose, all you need is a little resolution and...'

'No, no, I'm sorry, I—I couldn't.'

'Well,' said Lavinia, 'ask your brother to write a note apologising and you can give it to the man, whoever he is.'

'Oh, no,' said Rose. 'And—and Ferdy isn't very good at writing and—and...'

'Why don't the three of us go,' interrupted Edward, getting tired of the whole business. 'If I'm there it will be all right. We'll take no maids as they talk. Then the three of us can go in and face this man together and you, Rose, can tell him and that's all there is to it.'

'I really couldn't,' said Rose. 'I get so nervous when I'm faced with...'

'Oh, for goodness sake, Lavinia,' said her exasperated brother, 'you do the deed. Rose will just make a mull of it. If the gentleman is in, it will only take a minute to tell him and if he's not we'll write him a note.'

'Yes, very well,' said Lavinia, 'let us leave it at that. The next thing we have to do is to tell our parents a suitable story to enable us to go out without them, otherwise we shan't be able to go. Any ideas, either of you?'

'Well, I have thought of that,' said Rose proudly, surprising the others. 'It is Mama's birthday soon and Papa asked me to buy her a little brooch for a gift, you know. Could you invite me to go out with you, do you think? I'm sure Mama will let me go. You could tell your mama after we had left that it is to purchase a birthday gift for my Mama.'

'My Mother will wonder why I'm going with you, though,' said Edward.

'But you have to hire us a hack,' said Lavinia.

'Oh yes, of course.'

It was arranged between them that they would call for Rose at eleven o'clock the following morning.

Rose, smiling her thanks, returned to join her mother.

It wasn't until after Rose and her mother had left that afternoon that Lavinia told her Mama what they had planned, or part of it. 'You see, Mama,' she explained, 'I couldn't ask you in front of Rose's mama otherwise the birthday gift wouldn't be a surprise. For once, Edward said he would be obliging and go with us so that he can hire us a hack.'

Mrs Meadows nodded and said that Lavinia had arranged things well and she was particularly pleased her son was being helpful. Apart from saying that she hoped Rose was taking a servant with her, she was pleased to think her children were being resourceful and helpful to their less fortunate friend.

Lavinia breathed a sigh of relief and just hoped Edward and Rose didn't refer to the trip to Grosvenor Square at a later date.

In bed that night Lavinia thought about the following morning. She wasn't looking forward to it but she had promised to help her friend and she would go through with it. But she thought that if a similar episode was forthcoming from Rose's brother, they would have to find a way of dealing with it themselves. She wondered who this man was and why he had found it necessary to go to the length of calling out such a very young man. Would he have killed him? Perhaps they both had been drinking hard and didn't know what they were really doing. And was this unknown who they had to meet tomorrow an old man and a drunkard? The thoughts of this repellent subject swirled around in her brain until, mercifully, Lavinia fell asleep not to wake until the following morning.

She sat down to breakfast as usual, and although she wasn't looking forward to what she had promised to do, consoled herself that the three of them had only to deliver the news of Ferdy being underage to whoever this man was and then leave. Then she could relax and enjoy helping Rose to choose a brooch for her mama.

The wind had dropped overnight and although it was still cold, Edward suggested, as Rose lived reasonably near, in fact just round the corner, they could walk to her house and then hire a hack. Edward explained later that he had heard his father saying to his mother that the children could borrow their own carriage as no one else would be using it that morning and Ben, the driver, would take them to wherever they wished to go. So Edward had to tell a small lie saying that Rose wanted him to hire a hack from her house.

'You know, Vinny, helping other people is all well and good but when you have to tell lies to your parents it's another matter. If we had taken our carriage Ben would have probably told Papa where we'd been.'

'Never mind,' said his sister, 'I shall be careful in future I don't get involved in helping Rose out again.'

There were no more problems so just before eleven o'clock Lavinia and Edward set off for Rose's house where she was waiting for them.

The hack was hired and the address given to the driver. They settled back on the seats to be taken to Grosvenor Square.

'Did you find out the man's name we are to visit?' asked Lavinia.

'Oh, yes,' said Rose. 'Ferdy wrote it down for me.' She hunted in her reticule and brought out a slip of paper. 'Here it is,' said Rose. 'Sir Nicholas Sinclair.'

CHAPTER FOUR

THE JOURNEY to Grosvenor Square was of short duration. Here they found no street sellers shouting their wares or even anyone hurrying about their business. It seemed unnaturally quiet, the only person they saw walking very carefully with the aid of a stick, was an elderly military gentleman.

The driver asked Edward for the number of the house where he was to stop but as none of them knew where Sir Nicholas lived, Edward was the only one who could possibly alight from the carriage and enquire at one of the houses. Having done this, much against his will, the carriage was able to move on to stop outside number nine. The house was large and as they alighted Lavinia noticed how quiet and peaceful it all seemed. She also saw how the windows shone, that the paintwork was perfect and the steps leading to the front door were freshly brushed and cleaned.

They trod carefully up the steps and Lavinia felt quite awed at the prospect of entering such a house. She also felt, in her heart of hearts, that she would like to turn around and walk away. She pulled herself together and gave herself a mental shake. What was there to be frightened of? All they had to do was to say 'Good morning,' and give Sir

Nicholas the necessary information. Anyone could do that, she thought. She made sure her bonnet was straight and nodded to Edward to lift the knocker. The door opened immediately to reveal a liveried and bewigged footman who enquired their business.

'Please may we see Sir Nicholas?' Lavinia asked in what she hoped was a businesslike voice.

The door opened wider and they were invited inside and the footman pointed to the row of chairs lining one side of the entrance hall. They sat down and looked at the ornate mirror surrounded by portraits on the opposite wall. There were elegant branches of candles too, on the marble topped side table. Obviously this Sir Nicholas was a wealthy man.

'We shan't be long,' said Edward in a whisper. 'It will soon be over.'

'I—I don't think I can face this man or his wife,' said Rose. 'I am really frightened. Everything is so grand.'

'You will have us both with you and I will speak to him if you wish me to,' said Lavinia, but thinking it wasn't really her business.

'No, no, I couldn't, speak to him, I mean. I—I feel faint. I can't move, I—I...'

'Oh, very well,' said Lavinia, beginning to be annoyed. 'Edward and I will go.'

'No, no, don't leave me. Lavinia, stay with me.'

Edward glared at her.

'But Edward shouldn't go in—he has nothing to do with it. He was kind enough to accompany us, that is all.'

'Please,' said Rose, her face white and trembling.

'Oh, very well,' said Lavinia. 'Now we are here someone has to see Sir Nicholas. I'll go by myself. He can't be such an ogre as you make him out to be, Rose.'

An elderly but spry gentleman dressed in black came into the hall from the nether regions of the house.

'Good morning,' he bowed. 'Who wishes to see Sir Nicholas, please?'

'I do,' said Lavinia.

The man looked searchingly at her and asked Lavinia her name.

'I am Miss Meadows.'

'Thank you, Miss. Please come with me.' He stopped outside a large oak door and knocked. Whether a voice answered him Lavinia couldn't tell but he opened the door and announced her. 'Miss Meadows to see you, sir.'

Lavinia stepped into the most beautifully furnished room she had ever seen. Ornate rugs lay over parts of the polished floor. She could hear the ticking of the black and gold lacquered long case clock and see the embossed lacquer chairs and the gilt framed portraits and mirrors on the walls hung with deep maroon, ornate silk. The impression was of richness and beauty. She hurriedly looked round for Sir Nicholas and saw a figure lounging in a large chair with one leg hanging nonchalantly over one chair arm in front of a brightly burning fire. He was reading a sheet of paper, perhaps a letter. He didn't look up to see who had entered but said softly: 'You needn't wait, Roberts.' The man in black gave a small bow, looked anxiously at Lavinia and left the room, closing the door quietly behind him.

Lavinia still stood. Sir Nicholas went on reading. She looked at him and saw no elderly gentleman but a young man with very dark hair tied back. He wore a full sleeved shirt, open at the neck, and black breeches, white stockings and black shoes. His dark maroon coat was thrown over the back of another chair. She thought him rude as he went on reading while she stood and he didn't even hurry to dress himself properly in her presence. She wondered if she should say something but decided not to. As the clock ticked away she occupied herself by looking at the portraits on the walls of military men. Then she saw a very ornate framed picture of a beautiful lady above the fireplace and she was concentrating on this when a soft voice, quite near to her, said: 'Good morning, Miss Meadows.'

Lavinia jumped. How had he managed to move so quietly and quickly? He was only about three feet away from her. Now he was closer, she saw how tall he was, with the figure of an athlete. His face was certainly handsome, in that his nose was straight, his mouth sensuous and now faintly smiling, and his eyebrows were dark over nearly black eyes. Those eyes held an unpleasant gleam in them at the moment, Lavinia thought. Did he mean mischief? Was she safe? She gave a small curtsey.

Sir Nicholas noticed the worried but beautiful face framed by golden curls peeping from under her bonnet, the anxious blue eyes and the sweetly curved mouth. She was reasonably well dressed but could have looked better, he thought.

Lavinia began to feel more nervous. She pulled herself together. 'I have come...,' she began.

'One moment,' said Sir Nicholas, an amused look on his face, which Lavinia didn't quite like. 'Come closer to the fire, your nose is quite pink.' He held out his hand. His voice was pleasant.

'Th-that is because it is cold outside, sir,' said Lavinia, ignoring his hand, 'and I'm not staying.'

His smile grew. 'As you please,' he said. 'What is your name?'

Lavinia dared to heave a sigh. 'Miss Meadows,' she said impatiently.

'I know that. Roberts told me. What is your first name?'

'I don't see you need to know that, Sir Nicholas,' Lavinia said, beginning to be annoyed.

'But you know mine.'

'That goes with your title. I haven't one and...'

'So,' he interrupted, 'I shall have to think of one. Now it can't be Bluebell, they grow in woods. Now what grows in meadows? Cowslips, mm, not a very pretty name. Daisies? I know, buttercups. I shall call you Buttercup. So Miss Buttercup Meadows, why are you here?'

Thank goodness, Lavinia thought, not knowing how to cope with this silly kind of conversation. Now I can tell him and leave. 'I have come to inform you, sir, that the duel you are proposing to fight tomorrow cannot take place as your opponent is a minor and therefore by law is prohibited.'

Sir Nicholas smiled, but it wasn't a pleasant one. 'Really?' he inquired. 'And is he a friend of yours?'

'No,' said Lavinia, 'but he is the brother of a friend of mine.'

'So why doesn't your friend come and see me instead of you.'

'She asked me to come,' said Lavinia, wishing he would just accept what she said and stop playing games.

'I see. I think you have poked your nose in for some reason. So Miss Buttercup Pokenose, why have you come?'

'You are insulting, sir. Now if you'll excuse me...' She gave a little bob before turning.

He stepped forward quickly and caught her arm, turning her back to face him. 'You go when I say and not before. You've only just come. I think we should get to know one another,' he said, smiling down at her.

Lavinia began to be really frightened. She didn't like the way he was looking at her and he was standing too close. 'I don't think so, sir. I have told you why I am here, sir, now I must leave.'

'It was your idea to visit me. I didn't ask you to. You will leave when I say. Also I need recompense for the inconvenience of having this duel stopped. I was looking forward to killing that stupid young man.' He stepped closer to her until he was in front of her and Lavinia began to panic and automatically made to move back, but evidently he anticipated the move as he quickly grasped her wrists and whisked her arms behind her back and so held her in a vice like grip. He had a grin on his face. She was unable to move.

'Please...' she began and tried to struggle, which just made him hold her tighter. 'What would your wife think if she came in now?' This was all Lavinia could think of saying.

He laughed, which Lavinia thought sounded particularly heartless, saying he didn't have one, then lowering his head firmly fixed his lips on hers and kissed her. Lavinia didn't know where to look and she couldn't move away as he still held her. No one had ever kissed her before like that. Only Mama and Papa had kissed her, which now she knew was a different thing altogether. He looked amused and lowered his head once more. She tried to move away but he held her tighter as he went on kissing her. How long they stood there Lavinia had no idea, but she was beginning to feel breathless and weak although he was the one doing the kissing. The only thing she could think of doing at that moment was to kick him and somehow she managed to lift her foot and kick him on the shin. He relaxed his hold slightly, which enabled her to bring the heel of her little pointed shoe sharply down on to the top of his foot, and she pressed as hard as she could for good measure.

He jumped. 'You little wild cat,' he laughed, losing his hold on her. He tried to grab her again but Lavinia had had enough and managed to whisk herself out of his way.

'Now what do you think you deserve?' he said.

'I deserve an apology from you, Sir Nicholas.'

'I don't give apologies.'

'You are not a gentleman then,' Lavinia retorted.

With a laugh he quickly caught her again, lifted her bodily and carried her until they stood before the fire. She could feel the seductive heat on her back. It was a warmth that seemed to melt her. This time he took her gently into his arms, although she tried to resist him, which he overbore. He held her close and began to kiss her eyes, her nose and lastly her mouth, beginning gently and then becoming more demanding. His body felt hard, his arms strong. Lavinia had never known anything like it and felt herself succumbing to the demands of this man. Then as his hands began to move over her, her brain told her differently. 'No, no, no,' she managed as with a gigantic heave on her part she pushed him away.

'What are you afraid of, Miss Buttercup?' he laughed, ready to hold her again.

'You,' she said and managed with a final push to wrench herself away from him.

Fortunately for Lavinia, the door opened at that precise moment and Roberts appeared. 'What the devil do you want?' demanded Sir Nicholas, his brow darkening as he saw Roberts.

'I thought you rang, sir,' said Roberts, eyeing Lavinia's dishevelled appearance.

'You know I bloody well didn't,' snapped Sir Nicholas.

'Everything all right, Miss?' Roberts asked, looking at her pink face and her disarranged bonnet

'It is now,' she said, hurriedly straightening it. 'I shall try and forget your appalling behaviour, sir,' she said with what dignity she could muster. She walked past Sir Nicholas without another glance, into the entrance hall and as the footman appeared, nodded to the others who had been waiting for her. 'Come along,' she said, 'our business here is finished.' As the door was being held open she marched determinedly through it and down the steps, rapidly followed by the others.

After she had gone Roberts returned.

'Well,' Sir Nicholas said, 'has Miss Prim and Proper gone and why the devil did you interfere?' But Roberts noticed his spurt of bad temper had disappeared.

'Yes sir, she has gone. She was annoyed with you, I think. Did you...?'

'I'm annoyed with her. Do you know she kicked me?'

'There must have been a reason, sir.'

'Not as I know of,' Sir Nicholas said airily, with a cynical smile on his lips, 'and she said she would try and forget my appalling behaviour. I must pay her back sometime for hers.'

'Surely not, sir. She is a nice young lady, not like your usual ones. She didn't come alone. There was another young lady and gentleman with her.'

'Be careful, Roberts, you are on dangerous ground. But we shall see. By the way, did I have an appointment to fight a duel with some upstart tomorrow morning?'

'Not as I know, sir.'

'Then I wonder what she was talking about and why she came. Now leave me. I have a letter to answer.'

Roberts bowed and left the room with a worried frown, but he was pleased to see the black look on Sir Nicholas's face had disappeared.

Meanwhile, Lavinia, Edward and Rose were in a hackney going into town to find a jeweller.

'What happened?' asked Rose, seeing her friend was annoyed about something and that she had a dangerous gleam in her eyes. 'Was Sir Nicholas kind and is everything all right now?' she asked eagerly.

'Nothing happened and Sir Nicholas was horrid,' was all Lavinia said. 'But,' she added, 'everything is all right as far as your brother is concerned.'

'Oh, thank you,' said Rose, 'now we can be easy again.'

'Oh, can we?' thought Lavinia, still smarting under the disgusting treatment that Sir Nicholas had subjected her to.

Seeing the annoyed look in her eyes, Edward frowned. 'Did he make you angry, sis?'

'Yes,' said Lavinia, 'but I dealt with him. He is the most rude and horrid person. He's the kind that would pull the wings off flies, or—or anything. I shan't willingly see him again so tell your brother, Rose, not to deal with him.' She gave her brother a look that told him not to ask any more questions.

'Oh dear,' said Rose. 'I'm sorry.'

'Let's forget about it and go and choose a pretty brooch for your mama,' said Lavinia, still annoyed and sounding to Rose as if she was reprimanding her.

'Yes, Lavinia, thank you,' was all she could think of saying.

In bed that night Lavinia tossed and turned, going through what had happened that day. She was annoyed with Rose and her brother Ferdy and above all with Sir Nicholas. He was a disgrace to his name. How dare he treat her like that? Good gracious, even some boys she had known at home wouldn't have dared to do what he had done. She hoped she never saw him again in her life. He was rude, overbearing and a molester of women—well, of her at all events. She would have liked to have done a lot more to him than kick him. She didn't quite know what but if ever he did anything like that again she would think of something. And so, a restless Lavinia ended up with her thoughts in turmoil as well as the sheets, until her body and brain finally had had enough and she slept.

CHAPTER FIVE

THE NEXT MORNING at the breakfast table Mrs Meadows remarked on her daughter's pale face and tired eyes. 'I hope you haven't taken a chill, Vinny,' she said, looking anxiously at her.

'No, Mama, I'm sure I haven't. It is just that I didn't sleep too well. No doubt the cold weather is to blame.' She dare not look at her mother but she began to eat her breakfast so Mrs Meadows said no more.

'I think we should go and see how your new dress is progressing and then perhaps rest this afternoon as you, Papa and I are visiting Mrs Coombes this evening, if you remember. She kindly invited us and a few others she knows to hear a gentleman friend sing, so it should be a very pleasant and quite a restful evening.'

'If you're going to be out I shall read. What about you, John?' asked Edward.

'Could we play some games as well? I don't like reading for long,' moaned his brother.

'We shan't be leaving until about eight o'clock, so it will soon be your bedtime,' said their Papa. 'I'm leaving Edward in charge.'

John made a face at his elder brother but felt better when Edward winked at him.

Somehow Lavinia occupied herself all day until she and her parents arrived at Mrs Coombes's house. Lavinia suddenly thought how awful it would be if a certain gentleman was present there too. But she needn't have worried, for only one or two young people like herself, accompanied by parents, were invited. It was a pleasant evening, the gentleman who sang was amusing as well as having a rich baritone voice and he sang a varied repertoire to appeal to all.

During the days that followed, invitations to various friendly gatherings began to arrive. Lavinia's popularity was due, unknown to the Meadows family, mainly to Miss Euphemia Kelloe and Miss Drusilla Sonning. Hostesses relied on their opinions, especially on young ladies and gentlemen new to the social scene. Lavinia was approved of right from the start at Lady Winsley's first ball of the season, so her presence was automatically requested. Lavinia enjoyed all the attention and the many invitations she received, but wondered when she would have time to relax.

'You must make the most of all the opportunities given you,' said her Mama. And Lavinia, knowing how hard her mother had worked altering the dresses her sister had worn previously so that she had more than just the two new ball gowns, realised she must do her best. Some of the invitations she enjoyed very much, like the morning practice dances for young people. Lavinia found she had a natural ability and found dance steps easy to learn and remember, and she performed them with natural grace. At some of the evening gatherings there was music and singing and those talented enough (or merely confident enough) read their poems. But she tired of the readings of prosy older men and the singing of the castrati. To Lavinia's ears it sounded weird and unnatural, although most of the audience were enthralled.

There was no doubt that Lavinia was popular. She was pretty with manners to match. She would talk to shy young ladies as well as the hopeful young men. The hostesses complimented Mrs Meadows, telling her that her daughter had such sweet manners and was so pretty that it was a joy to invite her. Mrs Meadows was, of course, delighted, and told her husband that she thought it wouldn't be long before their daughter would meet someone suitable to marry. Meanwhile, she tried to keep a close eye on her.

And so the days and weeks passed by, the weather became slightly warmer, spring flowers began to appear in the parks and Lavinia looked forward to Lady Brigham's ball. Mrs Meadows had warned her that older people would be present as well as the younger ones and if an older gentleman asked her to dance she was to accept but not to dance more than twice with the same partner, whether young or old. Lavinia dutifully said: 'Yes, Mama,' but wrinkled her nose when her Mama wasn't watching.

In all this time Lavinia had seen little of Rose. Occasionally she was at a practice dance but they were all so busy joining in the quadrilles and cotillions that there was little time to talk. However, on one occasion during an interval when they sat drinking lemonade and chatting,

Rose artlessly said: 'It seems a long time since we went to Grosvenor Square, doesn't it? Do you know what my brother told me the other day?' Lavinia shook her head. Rose went on, 'He said we need not have gone.'

'Really?' said Lavinia, a frown on her brow. 'Why was that?'

'No,' said Rose, 'he said that he was drunk but he was very proud of the fact, you know, that he thought he'd challenged Sir Nicholas to a duel. But his friends told him he was so drunk he had dreamed it all up. Evidently he just went to sleep for a while. Silly, wasn't he?' Rose laughed.

Lavinia found herself nearly giving her friend a piece of her mind but managed to refrain. She wondered why Sir Nicholas hadn't said anything. He was even more despicable than she thought. And not only was she disgusted with Rose and her brother for involving her, she was now thinking of that arrogant gentleman again when she had nearly, not quite, but very nearly, obliterated him from her mind. What a fool he and Rose had made of her! Thank goodness he was never at the same evening gatherings to which she was invited.

Had she known, he easily could have been. Sir Nicholas was always popular and had more invitations than most people. After all, he was young, very good looking, a perfect dancer and a delight to watch. When he chose he could be kind and charming but this was seldom the case and he could be just the opposite if he felt like it. Consequently, people were a little afraid of him and some kept him at arms' length. This didn't worry him and he lost no sleep over it.

Most people were a waste of time, he thought. However, Roberts had noticed a minute change in him since that morning when Miss Meadows had arrived. But it was, perhaps, he thought, just wishful thinking on his part? Perhaps it was because she hadn't succumbed to his charms and she had rebuffed him instead and even had the audacity to kick him. Roberts, who had lived with Sir Nicholas all his life and had been secretary to Sir Nicholas's late father, smiled to himself. Perhaps Miss Meadows had taught this tiresome young man something.

Sir Nicholas still had friends, though. As he said once to Roberts: 'Where there is money, there are also friends.' He liked to visit the theatre and some musical concerts; he also fenced and visited the shooting gallery regularly. Horse racing was a passion, as he owned two thoroughbreds looked after in the stables of his country house in Surrey. He visited his clubs in London to gamble at faro or Black Jack and, because he could be charming to hostesses and he was a very eligible young man, he was invited to balls and social evenings, where, if he wished, he could be really delightful. If only he would be a little kinder, as his parents had been, thought Roberts, he would be the toast of the town. He shook his head and sighed.

As far as Sir Nicholas was concerned, whilst he still enjoyed his pastimes and his drinking sessions with his friends, he had become bored with his usual female company, trollops all of them. Yes, he remembered Miss Meadows and in one way had admired her but otherwise her attack on him, although she hadn't really hurt him, still riled him. He meant to pay her back in kind. At the social evenings he had honoured with his presence, she had been absent, but he could bide his time. He still wondered why she had really visited him. What was all that nonsense about a duel? But since meeting her, and he must admit she was a charming armful of which he hadn't held the like for some considerable time, he had felt different. He shrugged. He might never see her again. He was used to life's disappointments.

The day of Lady Brigham's grand ball arrived and Lavinia was excited. This was her first real ball, as she called it. She had been looking forward to it so much but now the time had nearly arrived she felt apprehensive. Her parents would be with her, of course, but from what she had been told the ballroom was of a magnificent size so she hoped she didn't become lost. She looked at her blue dress waiting for her, with which she and her mother were very pleased, as it was just what a young girl should wear. It was blue, the colour of the sky on a sunny day, thought Lavinia, and the sleeves and neckline (which was not too low) were edged with fine white lace. The underskirt of lace was decorated with tiny seed pearls and edged with a band of forget-me-nots. Mama had said that with a different underskirt it could be used many times, which would be useful. And for the first time she was to have her hair powdered and allowed one small patch on her face, possibly near her left eye.

Mrs Meadows found she had a dress of deep blue silk which she could wear and which her husband had always liked. He would wear a maroon, velvet coat with just a little lace at his throat and wrist and a patterned grey waistcoat. His shoes were black with silver buckles. He said he was too old to wear the latest fashions, and also this was his daughter's night and no one would bother about what he wore. Lavinia had laughed; she knew this wasn't true as both her parents were popular wherever they went.

Two important ladies, namely Effie and Dru, were also looking forward to the evening. They always arrived on time, as they liked to get settled before everyone else, they said. Also, they liked to see who came in, what they were wearing and make comments to each other accordingly. Lady Brigham had prepared for their arrival so they were escorted by a lackey to comfortable chairs amongst some potted palms and greenery, from which they had a good view of what was going on. They sat down, spreading their skirts and checking that their high elaborate wigs were secure. Effie's was decorated with mauve and purple flowers and Dru's had pink and red roses. Their faces, as usual, were powdered, and patches were placed at random, wherever they fancied. They had their fashionable painted rosebud lips, and long dangling earrings that nearly reached their plump shoulders.

'This is a good position, Dru, isn't it? Dear Lady Brigham knows just what we like, doesn't she? Oh, look, who's that who has just arrived? A macaroni with his white face and patches and he walks carefully on his high heels, too. Who is it?'

'I think,' said Effie, 'it's old Sir John Wallis. He's still looking for another wife, you know. I wonder if he is going to dance in those high heels?'

'I hope not. He's tottering now. Lady Brigham would be mortified if he fell over,' said Dru.

'So would Sir John,' giggled Effie. 'He still uses maquillage to hide his wrinkles. Look.' Indeed, Sir John's white painted face and patches shone in the candlelight.

'I prefer his wrinkles,' said Dru.

'Naughty,' admonished her friend, shaking her finger. 'Oh, look how pretty those Lindsay girls are and they are dressed prettily, too. They should soon find spouses.'

By this time the orchestra was playing softly as more guests began to arrive. A group of young ladies were trying to attract attention to themselves by laughing loudly and making use of their fans to signal messages to prospective partners.

'Mmm, those girls over there are rather noisy, aren't they, dear?' said Dru. 'Lady Brigham won't like that.'

'Trying to attract attention. Oh, look, two of their Mamas have reprimanded them.'

And so the two ladies were entertained by everyone coming in, noting what they wore and how they behaved. They would decide who they voted the belle and beau of the ball later when they had had a chance to see them dancing.

'Oh, look, Effie,' said Dru, vigorously fanning herself as the room became hotter, 'isn't that the little Meadows girl? Oh yes, it is. She is with her Mama, oh! and her Papa too. How sweet she looks. A nice family, I should think.'

'Yes,' said Effie, 'she's curtseying to Lady Brigham.

What a pretty child she is. I wonder if her nature is as sweet as she looks?'

'By all accounts she is quite popular,' said Dru. 'I expect this is her first grand ball. At least she doesn't push herself forward. Oh look, they've found someone they know. Her parents look kind and sensible people.'

'Do you remember her elder sister two years ago?' asked Effie.

'She wasn't as pretty, though, was she, Eff?'

'No, but she was soon happily married. So I expect this little one will be the same.'

'We shall see, won't we?' said Dru, bending down as best she could over her plump stomach to unhook the edge of her skirt which had caught on the heel of her shoe.

'Now you'll be pleased, Dru. Look, quickly, oh do be quick!' Effie poked a fat elbow into her friend's side and pointed with her fan to the figure who had just entered.

'Who, what, where?' gasped Dru, looking up quickly. 'Oh, yes, I see,' she said slowly, heaving a large sigh and continuing dreamily: 'Oh, yes. I do see. It's Naughty Nick.'

CHAPTER SIX

IT WAS INDEED Sir Nicholas and it was no wonder Dru looked dreamily at him with a sigh. His elegant figure was shown off to advantage, as he was dressed in a coat of gold and cream brocade with an embroidered waistcoat in old gold beneath. The finest Mechlin lace showed at his throat and wrists and his shapely legs were encased in cream stockings with golden clocks. Gold buckles were on his shoes and to finish his appearance his hair was powdered which showed up his dark eyes and brows. He looked the epitome of fashion and everyone's idea of a fairy-tale prince.

If he realised he had caused a stir he showed no sign of it as at that moment he was bending over the hand of his hostess, Lady Brigham. She touched him lightly on his hand with her fan as he looked up laughingly at her.

'Sir Nicholas, welcome,' she said.

'Dear lady,' he replied promptly, his face full of mischief, 'thank you so much for inviting me and may I have the very first dance with you?'

'I shall be honoured, sir,' she replied primly, belied by the smile in her eyes. 'There are many here who you know, I believe, and many who wish to know you.'

'And there are many I don't wish to know and there are

many who I wish would just go away,' said Sir Nicholas with that attractive grin.

'Naughty,' laughed Lady Brigham, rapping him over the knuckles as she moved away to welcome the next guest.

Nicholas was aware of many eyes following him and thought it all very amusing. There was a hush as he stood surveying the room at large through his eyeglass. While the young men looked at him enviously or disgustedly, depending on their nature, most of the young ladies sighed and hoped he would read their messages as they moved their opened fans into their left hands, signalling for him to come and talk to them, or they held them in front of their faces, showing they were desirous of his acquaintance. He didn't respond in any way, much to the young ladies' disappointment, but his eyes swept over the assembled figures, searching, searching. And then he saw her. Miss Buttercup. She seemed unaware of his presence as she was talking to a young man with two other young ladies. Nearby, older ladies sat who looked like mamas or duennas. Sir Nicholas didn't think how pretty Miss Buttercup looked or that she was holding her fan shut as she talked to the young gentleman. All that registered was that he had found his quarry at last. The evening promised to be interesting. As he lowered his eyeglass, conversation was continued once more. Two young men left the crowd and approached him.

'Sir Nicholas,' they said and bowed.

He turned. 'Thank goodness,' he said with a smile, 'there is someone I know.'

They laughed as they joined another group of young men who were evidently friends.

Some minutes later the orchestra began to play for the dancing. A gavotte was the first dance and Sir Nicholas went in search of Lady Brigham to lead the line of couples.

Lavinia's partner was the young man Sir Nicholas had seen her talking to and he was Lady Winslow's nephew, John, whom Effie and Dru had thought the most promising young man at the ball. Lavinia, of course, had met him at the practice dances they both attended and they felt comfortable with each other insomuch as they both knew the moves and steps. They were dancing in a different line of couples to Sir Nicholas, for which Lavinia was thankful. She had noticed he had arrived but as he mixed with a different set of people to herself she wasn't too worried

The gavotte was a charming dance. It was also lovely to watch. The first couples performed their dance steps then returned to the back of the line while the next couple danced. And so it proceeded with continual movement from one couple after another. Also the colourful apparel of the dancers added to the charm. Lavinia's mother, seated next to the other mamas, thought her daughter danced well and with flair. Lavinia's father had absented himself from the ballroom saying he was too old for dancing and had joined like-minded gentlemen in another room where conversation and cards were the entertainment.

So, as Effie and Dru watched, the ballroom was full of movement, colour and music with a background of voices and laughter, and they beat time to the music with their fans and remembered their own dancing many years previously.

Mrs Meadows also enjoyed watching, but after noticing

that her daughter was behaving and dancing as she should, she turned to the other ladies. Unfortunately, one, Mrs Winter, had a daughter, Carrie, who was not dancing. It was a shame, thought Mrs Meadows, that although she was a nice girl, her looks weren't out of the ordinary and her teeth were quite prominent. Her mama's idea of a white gown didn't help her, either, as it made her look pale. It was all very well looking pure and innocent in the eyes of the world but there had to be something else, too, like taste or charm. They chatted as the dancing continued, and the temperature in the ballroom rose and fans were much in evidence.

Although Lavinia was conscious of Sir Nicholas's presence she began to forget about him and enjoy herself. Obviously he moved in different circles to her and knew other people, so it was unlikely he would bother himself about her, whatever he had said. He danced with people unknown to her and she felt reasonably safe from his recognising her. They hadn't come in contact with each other in the dances so far and Lavinia told herself that if she was unlucky enough to meet him in any, she would just treat him like any other gentleman she didn't know. At the moment all was well and that was all that mattered.

Sir Nicholas would have been surprised if he had known this. He felt sure Lavinia had seen him and he hoped she was worrying when he would speak to her. How devastating it would be for her if he called her Buttercup in front of her mama, if the lady sitting with the others was indeed her mother. He smiled to himself. What a lot of trouble he could cause her. His eyes wandered round the room. She was dancing again, this time a minuet with someone he had seen before. If Sir Nicholas's memory served him right, her partner was a Frenchman, Monsieur de Craon, but that was all he knew. Evidently he was popular with hostesses and was invited to their functions. He certainly was attractive as he was very fair, unusual for someone from the other side the water, but who he really was Sir Nicholas didn't know. Perhaps he could find out. Was he an impoverished gentleman come over to England to seek his fortune or was he just over from Paris to enjoy himself? To Sir Nicholas's keen eyes he wasn't what he would term a good dancer, which was unusual for a Frenchman, but on second thoughts he supposed not all the French excelled on the dance floor. He had no natural elegance but he was attractive. Little Miss Buttercup was enjoying herself tonight, though. Perhaps after supper he could rectify that.

An allemande came next, a charming dance consisting of graceful body movements and with the interlacing of arms. Sir Nicholas invited an older lady of his acquaintance to perform this with him much to the younger ladies' disgust. Dru would have been envious if she had seen. The dance finished and his partner was returned to her group of friends. Sir Nicholas heard his name and turned with a smile on his lips.

'Shall we go down to supper, Nicholas?' asked his friend Richard. 'Or did you wish to take some young lady down?'

'I'm quite happy with your company, Richard. Let us go before all these people converge in the supper room ahead of us.'

'I think two people already have,' said Richard, nodding in the direction of the potted palms.

Effie and Dru, with shoes in hand, were waddling carefully and stealthily to their special seats.

Nicholas grinned. 'Oh, those old Ballroom Belles. I wonder if there is anything left for us?'

'Really? As bad as that, is it?' said Richard. 'Why do you call them that? They don't look as though they would chime sweet music.'

'Not that kind of bell, numskull,' laughed Nicholas. 'If you shook them though, I wonder.'

'Oh, no, it doesn't bear thinking about,' said Richard, making a face of disgust, 'but I was only funning. I was wondering why you are not quite your usual self tonight, that's all. You seem on edge.'

'Let's eat,' said Sir Nicholas, determinedly.

Mr Percy Meadows knew his duty and joined his wife and daughter to take them into supper. John reappeared by Lavinia's side and asked her if he could escort her, and Mary Meadows asked the ladies with whom they had been sitting to join them too. They were very pleased, as they had no gentleman in attendance.

The supper room was spacious with a large variety of food, alcohol and lemonade set out on tables, and while the ladies found a group of chairs the two gentlemen went to choose the wine and lemonade and delicacies from those on display. These included rich seed cake, heraldic devices made of tarts, cheeses, savouries in pastry, jellies, whipped syllabubs and, of course, refreshing ices. There was much chatter and laughter together with the rustle of skirts and the movement of heels on the wooden floor. Servants moved silently, serving wine, mopping up spills and offering more food. Eventually, with so many people the room became hotter and Lady Brigham's guests gradually began to return to the ballroom. Some windows had been opened during the supper break and the air felt fresher here but of course, the heat would soon return when the dancing began again. Most of the guests had reassembled in the ballroom and Lavinia and her mama returned to their chairs saying how much better they felt for the delightful refreshments. Percy Meadows returned with the other gentlemen to the card room, and the orchestra, also refreshed, began to play once more.

This time it was for a cotillion, a dance consisting of groups of four couples. They arranged themselves in a square and various dance figures were employed. As Lavinia looked up she saw Sir Nicholas approaching. 'Oh, good gracious,' she thought, 'he has seen me after all,' and she began to panic. She felt hot and then cold. She didn't know where to look so she gazed down at her fingers and tried to keep still. However, luck was on her side, Lavinia thought, and she let out a sigh of relief, when M de Craon cut across Sir Nicholas's path and stood once more before her requesting her to dance with him. She managed to accept gracefully and dared not look at Sir Nicholas.

Sir Nicholas, seeing what had happened, cursed the Frenchman under his breath, annoyed at him baulking him of his prey, but he tried to keep it from his face. He bowed before the other young lady, Carrie Winter, whom he thought looked insipid to say the least, but she would serve his purpose. If he couldn't partner Miss Buttercup, he could still be near enough her to teach her a lesson. He hadn't forgotten her kicking him. Miss Winter caught her breath at the honour Sir Nicholas did her by asking her to dance and she thought all the suffering and wishing to dance all the evening was rewarded by this one dance with Sir Nicholas, the best dancer by far in the ballroom. So it was a grateful and smiling Carrie who joined the set with Lavinia and her partner plus two other couples to dance the cotillion.

Sir Nicholas did not even glance at Lavinia and concentrated on what he was doing. Privately, though, he was thinking that when he passed Miss Buttercup in the Grande Chaine, he would contrive to trip her up, make her stumble and look ridiculous. Now this movement began and the dancers joined hands, the ladies turned to the left and the gentlemen to the right, and first with one hand and then the other they moved in a large circle until they met their partner again. But Sir Nicholas's plans went awry as in the movement before, Lavinia's partner, his brain perhaps a little confused with imbibing too much wine at suppertime, forgot the steps, turned the wrong way and collided with her, treading heavily on the top of her foot and somehow entangling his other foot in her dress.

There was a cry from Lavinia as an excruciating pain seared her right ankle and foot. She gasped. 'I'm sorry, I can't... my foot.' She stopped. Then she was conscious of her dress ripping as the Frenchman tried to untangle himself. She tried to hold her dress together and dropped her fan as she couldn't stand on her foot as it was so painful. All this happened in seconds but it seemed longer to Lavinia as she felt herself falling, falling. She automatically shut her eyes as she gasped: 'My foot, I can't...'

She heard Sir Nicholas's voice above her. 'Take my partner,' he said. Then she found herself lifted and carried out of the dance towards the potted palms, leaving Carrie to the mercies of the inebriated Frenchman.

CHAPTER SEVEN

EFFIE AND DRU were surprised, and to some extent pleased, to see Nicholas arrive. A lackey seeing the problem had the sense to provide a chair on which Lavinia was carefully placed.

'Do you require anything else, sir?' he asked.

'Yes, wine,' said Sir Nicholas, looking at Lavinia's white face. He turned to the ladies. 'You stand in place of a chaperone, ladies, if you please. Miss Meadows has had her foot trodden on and I must ascertain if anything is broken.'

'Oh, Sir Nicholas, of course, we're only too happy...' enthused Effie.

'Poor Miss Meadows, she looks very ill,' ventured Dru.

Lavinia indeed felt ill. Her foot and ankle were screaming with pain and she couldn't think of anything else. To have it touched, especially by Sir Nicholas, frightened her. Would he turn this to good account and pay her back for kicking him? She managed a breathless: 'Please don't,' as a tear found its way down her cheek. She hurriedly brushed it away with the tip of her finger. Seeing this, Sir Nicholas gave her his lace edged handkerchief.

'Look at me,' he said as he knelt down before her. His eyes held hers. There was no mischievous twinkle or cruelty there.

Lavinia managed to look at him through her tears. He didn't smile. 'I have to feel your foot to see if there are any broken bones. If there are you must visit the surgeon. I will be as gentle as I can, I promise.'

As Lavinia looked at him, she realised he was trying to reassure her. He seemed totally different to the Sir Nicholas of their previous meeting. She managed to nod her head.

He gently removed her shoe. This was a relief as her foot and ankle were found to be very swollen indeed. Little by little Sir Nicholas felt the bones and ignored her gasps when he touched a tender spot.

The lackey brought four glasses of wine, much to Dru and Effie's delight. One was given to Lavinia who refused it.

'Take it and drink it all,' said Sir Nicholas, 'it will do you good.'

'But I don't usually drink wine,' said Lavinia.

'You don't usually hurt your foot, so drink,' ordered Sir Nicholas firmly.

Effie and Dru grinned at each other.

'Mama...' began Lavinia.

'She shall be found in a moment,' said Sir Nicholas, and pressed on a very delicate part of her foot.

'Oh, please don't,' Lavinia gasped.

'That is the worst part, I think, but there don't seem to be any bones broken, though, after all, as far as I can tell. So,' said Sir Nicholas, getting to his feet, 'it's a cold compress for you, I'm afraid. It is painful but it will soon improve.'

'Th-thank you,' said Lavinia. She looked as white as the lace on her dress.

'Drink your wine,' said Sir Nicholas.

She took another sip.

'All of it,' commanded Sir Nicholas.

Mary Meadows came hurrying in. 'I was told something is wrong…' she began, looking from her pale faced daughter finishing her wine to Sir Nicholas standing in front of her.

'Dear Mrs Meadows,' began Effie, 'your daughter has had an accident and we are playing chaperones while Sir Nicholas is here.'

'I see,' said Mary. She went to Lavinia. She looked so ill that Mary was worried and took the wine glass away from her.

'What happened, Vinny dear?' she asked, bending over her.

'My partner trod on my foot, Mama, and has also torn my dress. Sir Nicholas says I have no broken bones, thank goodness. But I have broken your fan.' She tried to sound matter of fact but her voice broke and she had to fight back the tears.

'Can I be of any further help, Madame?' Sir Nicholas stepped forward. 'She should be taken home as soon as possible. May I suggest a cold compress? The wine will help her sleep.'

'Yes, of course. Thank you for your help, sir. If my husband could be found, please, I think he is in the card room.'

Sir Nicholas called the lackey back again who was hovering near. Giving him a coin, he told him to ask Mr Meadows to join his family at the main door as they wished to depart.

The lackey sped quickly away.

'But sir, how can I take my daughter to the carriage? My husband should be told to come here and...'

'It would give rise to curiosity, ma'am, which I'm sure you don't wish. I will carry your daughter to the door where your cloaks can be obtained and where your husband can join you.'

'Thank you, you are very kind. I must speak to Lady Brigham though, before I leave and tell her...'

'A message can be conveyed to her. It would make an unnecessary fuss to interrupt the dancing at the moment, I believe.'

'You are quite right, of course,' said Mary Meadows, not able to think straight and not quite knowing how to deal with these things. She wished her husband would hurry; it was just like a man to be absent when he was most wanted, she thought, unfairly.

They said goodnight to Effie and Dru, Sir Nicholas bowing and thanking them, which brought smiles of pleasure to their faces. Then, picking Lavinia up in his arms as though she weighed nothing, he headed through an anteroom to the stairs quickly followed by Mary Meadows carrying the rejected shoe. They reached the door below and it wasn't long before Lavinia's father came hurrying to them looking worried indeed. 'What has happened? What is wrong?' he asked.

'It is all right dear. Sir Nicholas has been most helpful. Call for our carriage, please, we must take Lavinia home.'

Upstairs, Effie and Dru were full of praise for Sir

Nicholas and sympathy for the poor little Meadows girl. What a thing to have happened! Sir Nicholas behaved just as he should, they said, even being so kind as to send for wine.

'Look, dear,' observed Effie, 'Sir Nicholas has left his wine untouched. Do you think he means to return?'

'I don't know,' said Dru, 'but it would be a shame to waste it. I know, let's share it. We can always hide his glass.'

'No, we might break it but if Sir Nicholas does return and he sees all the glasses empty, he'll think he drank it after all,' said Effie.

So as hurriedly as a plump and giggling lady could manage, Dru shared the wine between them and they sat back very well pleased with themselves.

Sir Nicholas hadn't given the wine another thought. After he had placed Lavinia in the Meadows's carriage, he had bowed, said goodnight and returned to the ballroom. He looked for Lady Brigham and was able to see her moving among the guests. He managed to speak to her and tell her of the Meadows's departure. When he had explained the situation, she thanked him.

'I didn't know you were so chivalrous, Sir Nicholas,' she laughed up at him.

'To tell you the truth,' he said, 'neither did I. I must be growing soft in my old age. I must return to my usual self.'

'Naughty,' said Lady Brigham, tapping him with her fan, 'but before you do would you oblige me one more time tonight?'

'Of course. Who do you want thrown out, that Frenchman?'

'Certainly not. He may have made a mistake while dancing but...'

'He was inebriated,' stated Sir Nicholas, bluntly.

'Well, let us leave him but could you please me by offering to dance with your previous partner. I saw she was upset. So would you, to please me, Sir Nicholas?'

It was the last thing Sir Nicholas needed to round off a ball that had promised to be so much fun. But he bowed to Lady Brigham saying with his usual charm: 'My only wish is to please you, dear lady.' And then he spoiled it all by adding, 'But why she has to have buck teeth like a rabbit I don't know.' He bowed and went in search of the unfortunate Miss Winter.

Home once more, Lavinia was carried up to her bedroom by her father, with an anxious mother following. Her maid, Selby, hearing Mr Meadows's voice, knew something was wrong and rushed up the stairs as she knew Mrs Meadows would need her. She was told briefly of Lavinia's accident and as the little maid, Betty, wasn't allowed to stay up so late, Selby assumed care of Lavinia as well. She tut-tutted over the torn gown and pursed her lips when she saw the swollen foot. 'Cold, wet bandages, Madame, and a few drops of laudanum, I think, to take away the pain,' she said, looking at Lavinia's pale face. 'But first we will undress you, Miss, and get you into bed. You'll be more comfortable there.'

Between them Mary and Selby managed this eventually, while Lavinia was passive under their ministrations. She felt too exhausted to do anything. Selby went away to find the bandages and laudanum while Mary went to tell her husband everything would be all right. She also found a stool to keep the bedclothes off the swollen foot.

In all this time Lavinia made no complaints or said anything. She felt very tired and everything that had happened since that last disastrous dance began to be mixed up in her mind. It was probably the wine, she thought vaguely, which she wasn't used to but she didn't really know. She did remember Sir Nicholas had been kind and caught her before she fell, and then had taken her to those frightening ladies. He had behaved so differently too, to when she had met him previously. Who was the real Sir Nicholas? Was he the womaniser or the serious person at the ball? Why was it important that she knew? She had no idea. She just thought she should know. She couldn't concentrate and her foot hurt so much that was all she could think of. She vaguely promised herself she would think more about this problem tomorrow.

By the time her Mama and Selby had finished bandaging her ankle, giving her a drink and settling her down to sleep, the hour was well advanced. Mary, feeling extremely tired, was helped to bed by her maid but was determined to visit her daughter later on in the night. Selby said there would be no need, as Miss would sleep well enough after taking the dose of laudanum she had given her.

Sir Nicholas, on the other hand, was still very wide awake. After dancing with Miss Winter to please Lady Brigham, he and Richard had taken their leave. They had gone their separate ways after making arrangements to meet later in the week. A sleepy lackey opened the door in Grosvenor Square and Sir Nicholas went straight up to his bedroom where his valet was waiting to help him prepare for bed. When this was done, Sir Nicholas asked him to fetch the decanter of port and a glass. He donned a warm and richly coloured dressing gown of crimson before finally sitting before the fire. The valet soon returned with the port and poured out a glass for Sir Nicholas, placing it and the decanter on a small table near him.

'Leave everything,' said Sir Nicholas, 'and you may retire. Goodnight.'

With a bow and a soft 'Good night, sir,' the valet quietly closed the door behind him.

Sir Nicholas sat staring into the fire with a frown on his face. Why had he done it, he asked himself? Why, when he was bent on making mischief, had he acted in the way he had? Was it because that damned Frenchman had done the deed and not him? But de Craon had hurt her, not on purpose perhaps, but she had been in pain. So why did he, himself, wish to inflict pain on Miss Buttercup? Well, he didn't really, did he? He had just intended to trip her up so that she looked ridiculous. This would have made her realise that she couldn't kick him when she felt like it. That was unworthy of him, he thought, a little guiltily. He looked at his port. Was it making him stupid? No, he didn't think so but little Buttercup had been in pain and she had tried not to weep. Also she had been frightened, hadn't she, when he began to feel for broken bones? Did she think he would deliberately hurt her? Yes, she did and that was why he had gone to all the trouble to be impersonal so that she wouldn't be frightened. He could see her white face now and the trickles of tears she had tried to suppress. A much different young lady to the one who had visited him before! He expected she would have been in trouble if he had mentioned her visit in front of her mother. For some reason this had been something she had decided to do by herself and not tell her family. She certainly had strength of character. He liked that. To be truthful he would have liked to have comforted and cuddled her. But why? What was it about Miss Buttercup that was different to all the others he had met? Perhaps her honesty plus a kind of inner quality. A long time ago, it seemed now, he remembered someone else like that and he had loved her dearly. It was his mother, and his father had comforted her in a similar situation.

Sir Nicholas sat staring into the remains of the fire for some time, then with a curse, he deliberately rose up from his chair, threw the remains of the port in his glass onto the fire and retired to bed cursing himself for being maudlin.

CHAPTER EIGHT

THE FOLLOWING MORNING, Lavinia awoke feeling tired due to the restless night she had had, in spite of the laudanum. Her foot was far from comfortable but she decided that after she had partaken of her hot chocolate, which Betty had brought her, she would feel much better if she arose from her bed as usual. She found that this was easier said than done but with the little maid's help, frequent sits on the bedside, hopping on her good foot and leaning on Betty, she managed to be dressed, deciding on a simple pink gown. Looking in the mirror she saw her face was pale but after Betty had brushed her hair and threaded a pink ribbon through her curls Lavinia thought she looked much better. There was a knock on the door. It opened and Selby came in.

'Your Mama asked me to look in on you, Miss, to see how you were. I see you've managed to dress. Shall I look at your foot?'

'Oh, Selby, thank you. It is still a little painful.'

Selby undid the bandages, remarking that it was still swollen, which was only natural but she thought it had improved from the previous night. 'I'll place fresh bandages on it, Miss, and I expect by tomorrow it will be much better, but you must keep it up as much as possible today.'

When Selby had finished, Lavinia's foot felt much easier. 'Now,' she said, 'how do I go downstairs?'

'You won't try, Miss, if you're sensible,' Selby said as she left the room, taking all the used bandages with her.

'I must go downstairs. I refuse to be cooped up in my bedroom all day. If I was ill it would be different, but I'm not,' said Lavinia. She tried placing her weight on her injured foot but found it wasn't a good idea and she had to sit down quickly to recover from the sharp pain. 'If I was at home I could slide down the banisters but here it's not so easy.'

'Oh Miss, you never,' said a scandalised Betty.

Lavinia grinned. 'I know it wasn't ladylike and I know Mama would not have approved if she had known, but it was fun. I'll show you one day when we are home again, Betty. I think John still does it on occasions.'

'Wait there, Miss, I have an idea,' and Betty left the room. A few minutes later she returned with two men servants, Martin, who served in the dining room and waited at table and George, who answered the door beside other work.

'They will form a seat with their hands, Miss, and carry you downstairs, if that is all right.'

'But my Father...?' began Lavinia.

'He is at breakfast, Miss,' said Martin. 'Now, if you can sit on the seat we've made and place one arm around our shoulders we can have you downstairs in a trice.'

'Let's try,' said Lavinia.

Carefully she was carried down with Betty tripping down before them and in next to no time they were in the hall. As Lavinia stood up she tucked a hand in each of the servants' arms and hopped, with their support, into the breakfast room.

'Good morning everyone,' she said as brightly as she could.

'Good gracious, I thought you would sleep late,' said Mrs Meadows, getting up.

'It's all right Mama, with help I have managed.' She thanked the two men. George pulled out a chair for her at the table and then left the room. Martin continued to serve the breakfast.

'How are you, Vinny?' Percy asked his daughter.

'I can't place my weight on my foot and it is still swollen but better than it was, I think, thank you Papa.'

'So no going out for you today then.'

'I'm sorry, Papa.' It sounded to her ears as though she had spoilt everything. 'Where were we going?' she asked in a small voice.

'There is no need to worry, dear,' said her mother. 'If you remember, we were going to visit our friends, Mr and Mrs Gilbert, in Hammersmith. Their boys are somewhere around Edward and John's ages. We thought it would be a change for the boys to have some friends to talk to. Your Papa and the boys can still go but I will stay with you, Vinny.'

'Oh, no, Mama. There is no need. You will want to see Mrs Gilbert. I can find something to occupy me, I'm sure, and Selby can take a look at my foot and Betty can get me anything I want.'

'Well,' said her mother, 'I suppose it would be all right,

if you don't mind. No doubt Sophy their daughter will be disappointed not to see you. She is about the same age as you, you know. Perhaps you could find time to write a few apologies to the invitations you have for this week. Perhaps next week's invites will be all right but no dancing for a while, Vinny.'

'No, Mama,' said her daughter with a sigh. Somehow, her appetite had forsaken her but as Edward and John decided to ask questions about the proposed visit to Hammersmith at this moment, no one noticed.

Two hours later Lavinia was alone. Her father had carried her into his study and her mother had found the invitations that Lavinia must decline. She sat and carefully wrote the notes of apology, some with regret, like the musical evening with an impromptu dance if enough young people attended. But evenings of poetry given by pompous old men who had an eye for young ladies, she could well do without. As she had nearly finished addressing the envelopes the knocker sounded on the outside door and a few minutes later George tapped on the study door.

'Come in,' said Lavinia.

'Excuse me, Miss, but a Mrs and Miss Smythe have called. Are you receiving visitors?'

'Oh,' said Lavinia, pleased in one way to have someone to talk to, 'yes, would you show them into the morning room please and I will...'

'Someone will come to help you, Miss. Just wait.'

After a few minutes Rose and her mother were surprised to see Lavinia enter the morning room holding on to George and Martin and hopping on one foot.

'Oh, my dear, what has happened?' asked Mrs Smythe.

'I'll explain in a moment. Would you like any refreshment, Ma'am?'

'Is your Mama at home?' asked Mrs Smythe.

'No, I'm afraid the rest of the family are out. We had planned to visit a friend but as you see I was unable to go.'

'Well,' said Mrs Smythe, 'if I may, I'll leave Rose with you. I know you will like to chat and you can tell her how you came to hurt your foot. Then I'll call for her on the way back from shopping in about an hour's time, if that is convenient?'

When Mrs Smythe left, Rose, looking neat but dull in a beige coloured dress, was eager to know how Lavinia had damaged her foot. 'We have missed you at the morning practice dance,' said Rose. 'Do tell me what happened. Have you broken it?'

'No, no, fortunately not. It is only a bad sprain, I think.'

'But how was it done?' persisted Rose.

'Well, I was dancing a cotillion and my partner forgot his steps and managed to tread on me. I—I think he had had a little too much wine at supper.'

Rose giggled. 'Who was it? Anyone I know?'

'The Frenchman, M de Craon. Do you know him?'

'No, but I've heard him spoken of. Tell me, is he handsome and dark?'

'No, not dark,' said Lavinia, 'in fact he's just the opposite.'

'That's odd for a Frenchie, isn't it?' asked Rose, disgusted. 'I thought they were all dark and handsome?'

'I don't know about that,' said Lavinia.

'Well, go on, what happened next?' asked Rose, smiling and hanging on every word.

Lavinia, for some reason, felt disinclined to go into detail about what happened, especially to Rose, who would probably ask questions as she knew, of course, of her first meeting with Sir Nicholas. All she said was that she was helped to leave the dance, her Mama and Papa came and she was taken downstairs to their carriage.

'Oh, poor you,' said Rose, disappointed that nothing romantic had happened.

'Never mind me, what have you been doing?' asked Lavinia, pleased to deflect attention from herself.

Before Rose could say they heard the doorknocker again.

'That surely is not Mama back so soon?' said Rose.

'No, I'm sure it isn't,' said Lavinia, 'now tell me…'

There was a tap on the door and George appeared carrying a small basket of primroses. 'This has just been delivered, Miss,' he said with a smile. 'It's for you.'

'Oh, how kind. Thank you.'

Rose noticed Lavinia's heightened colour and smile as she eagerly took the basket. She found a note attached. Her fingers shook slightly as she opened it.

'Who is it from?' asked Rose, all agog to find out if anything interesting was going on.

'Oh, it—it is from M de Craon.' Was there a look of disappointment on Lavinia's face, wondered Rose? But before she could say anything Lavinia was talking. 'Listen,' she was saying, 'it says: "I hope you are better now. Forgive me" and it's signed "R de Craon."'

'Well, that's something, I suppose,' said Rose. 'Do you like him more now?'

'It was kind of him to send the flowers but I don't think I like him any more than I did. Why?'

'I just wondered. Now I must tell you about this young man I've met. His name is David Banks. He came to the morning dances and he danced with me a lot and we became quite friendly. Then we met at an evening dance we were both invited to. Mama likes him and his family is not rich but they are comfortably placed, we're told. And the last piece of news is that Mama and Papa and I are invited to dinner next week. I don't know if Papa will be well enough to go, of course, but isn't it exciting?'

'Yes, oh, yes. I'm very pleased for you, Rose. Do you know how old he is?'

'Yes, he's twenty. Just two years older than I am.'

'Well, you must let me know how you go on from time to time, you know,' said Lavinia, attempting to be enthusiastic about the whole business.

'Of course I will. Perhaps when your foot is better and you go out more you will find someone you will like,' said Rose, trying to cheer Lavinia up.

'Maybe I shall,' said Lavinia, but without conviction. She had come to London for the season and she knew if she didn't find someone soon there was no money for an extra season.

After this, Rose continued to tell Lavinia all about David, what he looked like and what he said and thought. Rose was very pleased with herself and chatted on and on until Lavinia was tired of the name David, what he looked like and said and everything else about him. It was a relief when the doorknocker sounded and Mrs Smythe returned to collect Rose. She promised, when she could, to call again with all the up to date news. Lavinia managed to smile, thanked Rose for coming and shut her eyes in relief after the doors closed.

After a few minutes there was a tap on the study door. It opened and Selby entered saying that it was about time Lavinia's foot was looked at. 'And by the look of you, Miss, you're fagged to death.'

Lavinia managed to smile. 'My visitor was a little trying, Selby.'

'Mmm. Shall I call the men to take you back upstairs and then you could have a light luncheon and a little rest after I've dressed your poor foot?'

'Yes, I am feeling a little tired.' And depressed, she thought to herself. Perhaps after a nap she would feel more the thing.

It wasn't until nearly six o'clock that the rest of the family returned. By this time Lavinia was back downstairs in the withdrawing room awaiting them and feeling much better. The boys had thoroughly enjoyed themselves playing games with the Gilbert boys, and their parents said it had been lovely to see their friends again. When Lavinia had been asked what she had been doing, she was able to say that she had written her notes of apology as Mama had said, that Rose had visited and then Selby had dressed her foot after which she had rested.

'Oh,' said her Mama brightly, 'then you have done very well, my love. I'm pleased you had a friend to talk to and you received your lovely flowers. It wasn't such a bad day for you after all. Perhaps you will see the Frenchman a lot more at the dances. That will be nice. Oh, and while I remember, although Sir Nicholas was very helpful, dear, keep out of his way. He's not always as nice.' And she went out to see Selby.

'Yes, Mama,' said her dutiful daughter, thinking she had had the most boring day ever and she had no wish to see M de Craon at dances or anywhere else, or Sir Nicholas, for that matter.

CHAPTER NINE

THE DAYS that followed brought a little improvement to Lavinia's plight. Her brothers tried their hardest to amuse her and invent games to play. She was grateful and pleased that they cared about her and that her parents promised outings for when she could walk, but the trouble was that Lavinia had an active brain and she needed to be up and doing rather than sitting interminably sewing samplers. One day her mama was at her wits end to suggest something to amuse her daughter. The weather was pleasant and the sun, although watery, was out, making everywhere look much better.

'I wonder if you could manage to climb into the carriage, dear? Would you like that? I have a few shops to call at but at least you would be looking at something different to these four walls.'

Lavinia's face brightened. 'Oh, yes, that would be wonderful, Mama. I'm sure I can manage somehow, the swelling has nearly gone.'

'Well, try your shoes but if they are uncomfortable, keep your slippers on. No one will know if you keep inside the carriage.'

Lavinia was delighted that she would see other people

and breathe in some fresh air, not very fresh here in London, perhaps, but it would all be different to see. Perhaps they could enter the park?

She managed to put on her shoes with Betty's help. Her right foot still felt too large for the shoe but she was determined she would get into the carriage somehow. This was accomplished with the help of her father.

They set off and Lavinia noted with pleasure that the trees were looking fresh and green and the sky was still blue with just a few wispy clouds to make it interesting. How lovely everything looked even in London, when one hadn't seen it for a few days. Some stops were made for Mrs Meadows to purchase small items such as thread to repair a dress and some ribbons and then they turned into the park where more people were walking, riding and meeting friends.

'Oh, look, Vinny,' said Mrs Meadows. 'Isn't that M de Craon? I think you should thank him for his primroses and show you are not vexed with him.'

'But Mama...' Lavinia began.

'It is only polite,' admonished Mama.

'Very well,' said her daughter, but not very enthusiastically.

Mrs Meadows knocked to stop the carriage just a little way beyond where the Frenchman was walking with a friend.

As the gentlemen came abreast of the carriage Mrs Meadows let the window down. 'M de Craon?' she called.

He looked round, rather surprised to be addressed by an older lady but he bowed while his friend looked on.

'M'sieur, my daughter would like to speak to you, if you please,' she said, making way at the window for Lavinia.

She wouldn't really, thought Lavinia but she moved obediently to the window and summoned up a smile. 'M'sieur, I wished to thank you for my primroses,' she said.

The Frenchman smiled up at her and bowed once more. 'It is a pleasure to see you out, Mam'zelle. I trust you are now well?'

'Thank you, M'sieur, I'm very well.'

'I hope to see you at the dances, then, very soon when I hope I can make amends for the inconvenience I have caused you,' said M de Craon with a smile and a yet another bow.

Lavinia dutifully smiled while he stepped back and the carriage moved on.

'Wasn't he charming?' said Mrs Meadows. 'He speaks English very well, doesn't he? His French accent is very attractive, isn't it?'

'I suppose so,' said Lavinia, fast losing interest and looking out the window eagerly to see if anyone else was walking or riding whom she knew. But apart from knowing some of the ladies she had met at previous venues, Lavinia saw no one in particular.

It wasn't long before they were back home but Lavinia felt better for the outing.

'You know, dear,' said Mrs Meadows as they sat once more in the morning room, 'there are only a few weeks left before we return home. I think you should encourage M de Craon a little more. I know he didn't begin very well but he looks so very nice and behaves just as he ought.'

'Oh, Mama, how can you? He hasn't been anywhere near me apart from one disastrous dance and sending flowers. Besides, I don't care for him. I grant you that he is a little attractive, if you like fair haired gentlemen, but I couldn't marry him. Besides, we don't know anything about him—his background, I mean.'

'Your Papa could look into that but we shall have to see,' said her mother with a shrug.

Fortunately for Lavinia her mama couldn't say anything more as the door opened and her papa and brothers entered the room.

'Mama,' said John, rushing in big with news, 'we have seen the river and London bridge. Ugh! I wouldn't like to live near there. But there were some vessels on the water which were interesting and there were some children looking for treasure in the mud which I would like to do, but the smell in some parts was unbearable and I had to hold my nose and...'

'That will do, John,' said his mother. 'We are not interested in horrid things.'

'Tell me about it later,' whispered Lavinia as her mother turned to listen to what her husband was saying.

There was a knock on the door and George entered with a small envelope on a silver tray. 'This has just arrived, sir,' he said.

Mr Meadows took the note and opened it and quickly read it. 'Listen,' he said, 'this is from Mr Gilbert. He asks if Lavinia, her Mama and I would like to join them and their daughter in their box at the Drury Lane theatre tomorrow night. If we would like to go then we should all meet in the entrance.'

'Oh,' said Lavinia, 'please can we go? I should like that above all things and I can meet Sophy too, and I'm sure I can manage.'

'What do you think, Mary, my dear?' asked her husband.

'It is very kind of them and I'm sure it will be a suitable play otherwise they wouldn't take Sophy. I think we should accept. My friend's mama hires a box, I believe, and there would be room, no doubt, for another three people. And if we don't like what we see we can always leave, you know.'

'I will go at once and write our acceptance, then,' he said and hurriedly left the room.

'My foot is much better and I should be quite all right to go,' said Lavinia.

'And you'll be sitting down anyway and your Papa can always help you up any steps if there is a problem.'

'I wonder what we shall see, do you know, Mama?'

'No, but if it is Drury Lane it will be something quite special like a play by Shakespeare, with the best actors. There will be no music, though.'

'Why?' asked Lavinia, wrinkling her brow. She liked music.

'It is something about a Royal Charter granted by King Charles the Second, so only the best actors perform there. You must ask your Papa if you want more details,' said her mother.

Lavinia wondered why something granted by a king who lived over a hundred years ago was so important. It would still be fun to visit the theatre, though, and see a play and other people.

The next thing, of course, was to find a suitable dress.

'You know,' said Mrs Meadows, 'I think that cream one you wear in the evenings when we attend small functions would be suitable. You can wear your pretty pink necklace and earrings. After all, you will be sitting down so there is no need to decorate the skirt, as it is quite full. What do you think, Vinny?'

'Yes, and I could wear a flower in my hair too.'

Lavinia's apparel organised, Mrs Meadows went off to find Selby to request her assistance for the next day and the pressing of the dresses.

Lavinia was arrayed in her cream dress with its tight bodice, low neckline and full puff sleeves. She had long gloves to match and Selby had dressed her hair simply and pomaded her locks until they shone and in which she had fastened a sparkling comb with cream rosebuds to match her dress. When her mama saw her she was well pleased and said she looked very pretty.

'Thank you, Mama. But you look very nice too. I do like that blue dress and it suits you beautifully.'

'Well, let us go downstairs and dazzle your Papa.'

He looked very smart, wearing a white wig and dressed in a dark maroon velvet coat with black knee breeches. He told 'his ladies' as he called his wife and daughter, that they looked good enough to eat after which they happily set off in the carriage leaving behind two boys who planned the games they would play and the supper they would request.

The Meadows's carriage stopped near the entrance of Drury Lane theatre, which was fortunate as the evening was decidedly chilly and the ladies had only their shawls over their dresses. Everywhere was bustle, chatter and laughter. Flunkeys undid the carriage doors and let down the steps assisting the occupants to alight. The carriages then moved quickly away while the occupants ascended the stone steps of the theatre, pleased to reach the warmth of the entrance hall where the candles in the wall sconces and chandeliers glowed a welcome. It was noisy with everyone talking and laughing, meeting and greeting, and eyeing everyone else.

Mr Gilbert saw them and came forward. 'Good evening,' he said, bowing. 'We are pleased you could come. It is a long time since we all met, isn't it? And you must be Miss Lavinia,' he smiled. 'You were only tiny when I saw you last.'

Lavinia saw before her a gentleman of medium height, dressed in a blue coat and she looked up into a kind face as she managed a small curtsey while the crowds milled round them. 'Thank you for inviting me, sir,' she smiled.

'Come along then and meet my wife and daughter.' He led the way to where they were sitting on two small chairs in a corner but they arose immediately they saw their friends approaching. After introductions they climbed the stairs, Lavinia ascending very carefully, to find their box. She walked with Sophy who was a year younger than herself. She seemed a quiet girl but pretty with dark hair, and dressed in a lovely gown of soft pink silk. She was friendly and as Lavinia was quite outgoing they were soon chatting away quite happily to each other.

The Gilberts' box was situated on the left of the auditorium on the second storey. It was reached by stairs and then down a narrow corridor that ran along the back of all the boxes. There were six chairs and Lavinia and Sophy were seated together in the front so that they had a good view. Their parents were seated together behind them but all could see the stage.

As Lavinia sat down she was aware of people in other boxes opposite and cast a quick glance across. She was surprised to see two ladies smiling and waving to her. 'Look Mama, those two ladies were with me when I sprained my foot at the ball,' she said, so she waved to them and smiled back.

'Oh, how sweet of her,' said Effie, 'she remembered us. Now I wonder who she is with, besides her parents?'

'Well, that is old Mrs Gilbert's box so perhaps the others are her relations, dear,' replied Dru.

'Mm, the little Meadows girl is creating a sensation in the pit, isn't she? And perhaps her little friend is as well,' said Effie.

And indeed they were right. The beaux of the town were walking about ogling the pretty girls through their eyeglasses. Those in the boxes on the lower tier had an uncomfortable time of it unless to be seen was their real reason for visiting the theatre. Apart from being looked at, it was the continual laughter and loud voices of the young men that must have been hard to tolerate.

'Is our other young friend here tonight?' Dru looked

from left to right. 'I don't see him,' she said, looking down.

'My dear,' said Effie, 'he won't be down there. Does he have a box here, I wonder?'

'Of course, you're right. Sir Nicholas wouldn't mix with the hoi polloi, would he? Perhaps he has friends who have a box if he hasn't. But can you see him liking Shakespeare?' asked Dru.

Effie shrugged. 'It makes a nice evening out anyway, don't you think?'

Lavinia began to get used to being looked at by the bucks walking in the pit and was able to look at the theatre itself with the ornate decorations of cherubs and red plush. She found Sophy friendly and quiet and wondered if she was always like it, or was she on her best behaviour because she was with her parents? But she was a nice girl and Lavinia hoped to see her again.

The boxes were all full with elegantly dressed ladies and gentlemen, some of whom had come to see the play, but others who had come only to be seen. The latter were wearing eccentric fashions, which made walking and even sitting, difficult. They had high standing wigs below which were their rouged and patched faces.

It was nearly time for the curtain to rise when there was a movement in the box opposite. It contained three young men who sat quietly talking and looking at the rest of the people gathered there. Lavinia thought she had seen them somewhere before, probably at one of the balls she had been to. Now the door opened at the back and the figure of Sir Nicholas appeared. It wasn't that he had entered noisily but his friends stood up and clapped and gave him quite a welcome. Obviously they hadn't expected him to arrive for some reason. Why, of course, was not obvious to everyone else. The four gentlemen quietened down and they perused their programmes while Sir Nicholas took his seat, looking around as he did so. He observed the bucks in the pit and the people in the boxes.

Lavinia had by this time averted her gaze and was talking to Sophy. Was the temperature in the theatre rising, or was it just her seeing Sir Nicholas that had caused her flush?

Then Mrs Meadows leant forward. 'Here is a programme, Vinny. See, the name of David Garrick is at the top. He is playing the lead of the Duke. He is supposed to be a most excellent actor, you know. Would you like to share this programme with Sophy?'

'Thank you, Mama,' said Lavinia.

The two girls looked at the programme and made a pretty picture, although neither of them knew any of the names of the players.

'Oh,' said Sophy, 'it says Orsino, Duke of Illyria. Where's that, Lavinia, do you know?'

'No, perhaps Shakespeare just made it up. Oh, look there are some funny names, aren't there? Sir Toby Belch, that sounds rude, and Sir Andrew Aguecheek.'

Sophy giggled. 'We had better not point them out to our Mamas, had we? It's not ladylike.' They looked at each other, laughing.

This wasn't lost on Sir Nicholas sitting opposite who wondered what had caused them to look so mischievous.

As if aware of his attention they looked across at him. He inclined his head and smiled. Lavinia gave a quick smile and, with her Mama near, hurriedly looked at the programme again, while Sophy gasped as she looked at Lavinia.

'Who is it?' she whispered. 'Isn't he handsome? Do you know him?'

'I have met him briefly,' was all that Lavinia could think of saying.

Then fortunately, a bell sounded to tell everyone the play was about to begin. All was quiet and the audience looked instantly at the stage, until a disturbance occurred and everyone's eyes were drawn to the figure of a tall young man in the pit. He stood beneath Effie and Dru's box, his face upturned. He decided to attract their attention by calling obscenities to them. While everyone was shushing everyone else, Effie and Dru, never at a loss and without the least hesitation, picked up from the floor a large jug of what might possibly have been lemonade and poured it onto the tall young man's face. He began to splutter, while the two ladies resumed their expectant demeanour, looking at the stage and vigorously fanning themselves. Meanwhile, the now sodden young man, amid guffaws, was escorted out of the theatre.

CHAPTER TEN

IT WAS THE INTERVAL. The curtain had descended and the ladies in Mrs Gilbert's box heaved a great sigh. Lavinia and Sophy sat staring before them.

'Well,' Mrs Gilbert's voice said behind them, 'what do you think to your first visit to Drury Lane theatre, ladies?'

'Oh,' said Lavinia, 'wasn't it wonderful? How do they manage to remember all the words, I wonder.'

'Yes, and the costumes were so pretty, too,' put in Sophy.

'We had better make the most of the time now,' said Mrs Gilbert, arising from her chair. 'I see our gentlemen have already left the box, so do come and walk with me, Mary, otherwise we shall be so stiff. You two may come with us if you wish.'

But apart from standing up the two young ladies went on praising the actors and expressing their preferences to each other.

'I liked the one who sang, he had a pleasant voice. His name was Feste, wasn't it? A funny name,' said Sophy.

'Oh yes, but Olivia was nice, wasn't she? And I would love to be Viola,' mused Lavinia dreamily.

They were brought down to earth by a knock on the door of the box. It opened and a young gentleman stood there. 'Oh,' said Sophy, blushing, 'I didn't realise you were here tonight, Martin. May I introduce my new friend to you? Miss Lavinia Meadows.'

Martin duly bowed and Lavinia, seeing her friend pleased to see this young man, said: 'Do take my seat, sir. I would like to continue to stand a while.'

Lavinia moved to the back of the box. Martin was pleased to take his seat next to Sophy and they were soon chatting and discussing the play.

The door opened once more. Sir Nicholas stood there. 'Good evening, Miss Meadows,' he said, bowing slightly. 'Are you enjoying the play?' As he said this he noticed the young couple were well into their conversation while Lavinia, somewhat breathless at the sudden appearance of Sir Nicholas, gave a small curtsey and managed to say: 'Very much so, sir. And you?'

'Come into the corridor and we can talk and walk there.' He held out his hand and Lavinia automatically laid hers on his. He drew it through his arm and they went into the corridor at the back of the boxes. 'How is the foot?' he asked.

'Much better, thank you, apart from it becoming stiff if I sit too long.'

'Like now,' he said.

She looked at him with a smile. 'Like now,' she confirmed.

'Then I'm performing an act of mercy?'

'Indeed you are, sir,' and spoilt the prim reply by giggling.

Sir Nicholas's lips twitched. 'You weren't laughing last time we met,' he said.

Lavinia became serious. 'No, sir, and I don't think I thanked you properly for helping me. At the time I was in pain and that is all I could think about and I haven't seen you since,' she finished.

Sir Nicholas suppressed a smile, noticing the hurt note in her voice. 'You have nothing to thank me for, Miss Meadows.'

Lavinia said nothing. She didn't know what to say.

'And have you more balls to go to? Will you be able to dance?'

'I hope so. I plan to go to a practice dance, they are held in a morning, you know. Then if I can, I shall go to the balls to which I've been invited,' Lavinia finished sedately.

'And have you been invited to Lord and Lady Waverly's ball?'

'I don't know, sir. Mama hasn't said, but I hope so.'

'Then I shall see you there.'

'I shall look forward to it.' As she said this she looked up at him, wondering if he had an ulterior motive. She never knew if he was serious or not.

Sir Nicholas wasn't so delighted with the considering look she gave him. She seemed as though she still did not trust him entirely

'And will you dance the first minuet with me?' Sir Nicholas enquired.

'Thank you, sir, I shall be delighted,' she replied.

The bell sounded which heralded the next act so Lavinia and Sir Nicholas turned and walked back to the box. Sophy's friend was just leaving so he joined Sir Nicholas and they walked away together while Sophy thanked Lavinia for giving Martin her seat. Lavinia said nothing but sat down and hoped her parents hadn't noticed Sir Nicholas.

But Mrs Meadows had certainly noticed and gave Lavinia a hard stare as they all took their places again. Lavinia, painfully aware of her mother's eyes upon her, immersed herself in looking at the programme and pointing out the next act to Sophy. Under cover of this pretence Sophy whispered, 'Doesn't the gentleman you saw sit in the box opposite? He's very handsome, isn't he? Have you met him before?'

'Yes,' whispered Lavinia, 'but Mama isn't very happy about it.'

'Oh, I'm so sorry,' said Sophy, pointing at the programme with one finger.

No more was said as fortunately for Lavinia the audience had become quiet and the curtain was raised once more to show the final act of the play.

There was loud applause as the play ended with a standing ovation for Mr Garrick. When the curtain finally came down the business of gathering personal things and chatting while making way to the stairs was like a douche of cold water to Lavinia. She would have liked to have sat and just stayed in the story of the play for a while. But the two mamas were hurrying their daughters along as goodbyes must be said and carriages found. Sophy hurried with her mama as she was bid, followed by Mrs Meadows. Lavinia tried to keep up but her foot had gone to sleep and felt stiff so she trod carefully. If she could get to the handrail she knew she could manage. She tried to work her way through the crowd to the side but no one knew of her plight and just gave her rude stares. So she waited, standing to one side and as the crowd lessened she moved carefully towards the handrail. She had negotiated the first steps when she gasped as a strong arm encircled her waist, lifted her completely off her feet and carried her down the rest of the steps, depositing her carefully at the bottom. It was Sir Nicholas, of course. No other would have dared do it. Was he trying to make trouble for her?

Lavinia didn't know whether to be pleased or sorry. If her mama had turned and seen him she wouldn't have liked it one little bit. But Lavinia was so relieved that she was down the stairs safely that she turned to Sir Nicholas with a smile. 'Oh, thank you,' she said, 'my foot is stiff again, I'm afraid.'

'I thought it might be.'

'Gracious, it's a good thing Mama didn't see,' she said.

What a pity she didn't, he thought. Aloud he said: 'There was no one to help you. And no one looking to see if you were all right. What would they have said if they had seen you just now?'

'I hope they would have been pleased with your help for me but somehow I doubt it.'

He laughed but not pleasantly. 'And did you enjoy the rest of the play?'

'Oh yes, I would have liked to have stayed and seen it all again. Did you enjoy it, sir?'

'Of course, I did,' he smiled, looking down at her. 'Your

face was a picture of different emotions, you know.'

Lavinia blushed but looked severely at him. 'Then you should have watched the play, sir. The acting was very fine.'

Sir Nicholas's lips twitched but he answered meekly enough. 'Yes, I know I should. I'm sure it was as you say.'

Lavinia looked quickly up at him. 'Are you laughing at me, sir?'

'No, little Buttercup, I wouldn't dare.'

Before Lavinia could say anymore Sir Nicholas with a laugh was bowing and wishing her good night.

So it was an indignant looking daughter that Mrs Meadows found as she looked round to see what had become of Lavinia. 'Do come and say goodbye, dear,' she called.

Lavinia pulled herself together, smiled, curtsied and said she had been pleased to have been invited, and especially to have met Sophy. They parted quickly afterwards, as their ears were assailed by the noise and bustle of people leaving, calling for carriages, shouting goodbyes, laughing and cursing their particular coachman for not arriving promptly. Eventually Lavinia and her parents were moving away at a great rate seated inside their carriage.

'You managed the steps then, Lavinia?' asked her mother.

'Yes, I did,' said Lavinia, pleased that in the darkness of the carriage her mother couldn't see her blush. 'It is stiff after I've sat awhile so I am slow. I think I had better go to a practice dance and see if it will help.'

'A good idea,' said her Mama, 'and perhaps Edward could go with you. He's been neglecting his dancing lessons since being in London.'

'And his fencing,' said Mr Meadows. 'I'll see if I can find somewhere for him to practice.'

And so the moment had passed and Lavinia breathed a sigh of relief that her parents had not seen Sir Nicholas again.

At breakfast the next morning Edward dutifully asked how the play had been and said he hoped to visit Drury Lane sometime. Lavinia said it had been a lovely evening and proceeded to tell them about some of the scenes.

'Pooh,' said John, 'sounds fusty to me with all those words. People would be better staying at home and playing games with their children.'

'Thank you,' said his father, 'when we want your opinion, John, we'll ask for it.' He hoped the reprimand might be all that was needed but it seemed to have no effect whatsoever as John continued with his diatribe.

'John,' said his Papa once again, laying down his knife and fork to give emphasis to whatever he was going to say. Edward quickly kicked his brother under the table.

'Yes, Papa?' asked John politely, but scowling at Edward and rubbing his ankle.

'For goodness sake eat your breakfast in silence,' his Papa snapped.

A short silence ensued which was broken by Lavinia who tried to take the attention away from her younger brother by asking her father about the Royal Charter her mama had told her about. 'What I don't understand,' she said, 'is that music and songs are not allowed but there was music in the play last night.'

'Yes,' said her Papa, pleased at least one of his children could speak about something sensible. 'But as they were written into the play they are allowed. I think what really matters is that if there were too many other songs and music it would detract from the quality and performance of such actors as Mr Garrick.'

'Oh, I see,' replied a doubtful Lavinia.

'So,' said Mrs Meadows, changing the subject, 'you are going dancing with Lavinia this morning, Edward, are you?'

'Oh yes, please do, Edward,' said Lavinia.

'All right, but what about John, Mama?' asked Edward, seeing his brother making a face at him.

'He can go with me and we can see if we can find a fencing school, can't we, John?' said his father, thinking that after his younger son's outburst he should include him in an outing. 'Perhaps we could watch some of the students there.'

John thought this a good idea so with every one organised Mrs Meadows was at liberty to visit a friend and hopefully the shops which she loved so much.

The young people at the practice dance that morning were already performing a country dance when Lavinia and Edward arrived. Mrs Williams welcomed them as usual saying she was especially pleased to see Edward as gentlemen were in short supply that morning. It wasn't long before Rose saw them so they went to sit with her. She dutifully asked after Lavinia's foot and said she was pleased to see Edward again. After that, although she took part in the conversation her eyes remained focussed on the door.

Exasperated, Lavinia asked her if she could possibly be expecting someone. 'Oh,' said Rose, 'I was wondering if David would be here this morning. He said he would come.'

'Then I expect he will arrive at any time,' said Lavinia, looking meaningfully at Edward.

'You had better dance with me first, Lavinia,' said Edward. 'This is a gavotte and I'm not sure of all the steps.'

'Well, kind sir,' said his sister with a laugh, 'how can I resist—but please don't tread on my foot.' And so they joined the dance.

'I couldn't think of anything else to say,' whispered Edward. 'She's such a bore, isn't she? And who is this David?'

'She told me about him when she visited me,' whispered Lavinia as they took their places in the line of dancers.

By the time the dance was finished evidently David had arrived, as Rose gave Lavinia a little wave with her fan and said as soon as they were near: 'Do let me introduce you to my friend David Banks. David, this is Lavinia Meadows and her brother Edward.' Bows and curtseys followed.

Lavinia saw before her a gangly youth of about nineteen but he seemed pleasant enough.

'Have you been to these dances before, Mr Banks?' asked Lavinia.

'Only twice,' he answered.

'He is such a good dancer that he really has no need,' laughed Rose.

David smiled a little. 'Practice hurts no one,' he said seriously. 'Shall we?' he asked Rose, holding out his hand as a minuet was announced.

Rose, tossing her head, was all smiles as she passed Lavinia, who didn't notice as a young man she knew from previous dances was inviting her to partner him so Edward was at liberty to choose whom he liked.

The next dance was a quadrille and David courteously asked Lavinia to dance.

'Oh, let us join them, Edward,' Rose said, quickly taking his arm. With another two couples they were ready to begin and it wasn't long before David was smiling at Lavinia and complimenting her on her dancing. 'You are so light and elegant,' he said. 'It is like dancing with a fairy.'

'I expect you dance with many fairies,' said Lavinia, laughing up at him.

'Quite a few,' he grinned, 'but never here until now.' They were separated in the dance so Lavinia was pleased, as she couldn't think of a suitable reply.

Rose wasn't pleased, though, as she noticed Lavinia and David were getting on well together and she didn't like it. She began to tease Edward rather loudly. He refused to answer her, thinking she was a dead bore and the sooner the quadrille finished the better. The other two couples looked at Rose but said nothing.

After two more dances Edward whispered to Lavinia that he would like to leave and return home. 'Rose is such a bore and I'm tired of both of them.'

'They are well suited,' Lavinia grinned. 'But, yes, let us go home. I've found I have no problem dancing again so we don't need to stay if you really wish to leave.'

When they told Rose and David of their decision Rose

said she was sorry but sounded relieved, whereas David looked genuinely disappointed. He bowed and said something about a fairy.

'What was that David was mumbling about?' Edward asked his sister as they left the room.

'He said he had never met a fairy like me before,' said Lavinia with a twinkle in her eye.

Edward looked disgusted. 'Which just shows what a stupid fellow he is. He and Rose are well matched, I think.' Lavinia nodded and laughed.

CHAPTER ELEVEN

'YOU'RE BACK early,' remarked Mary Meadows when Lavinia returned home.

'Yes,' said Lavinia, 'we found it tedious but my foot seems to be back to normal and Edward danced very well so there was no need for us to stay.'

'But didn't you see any friends?'

'Well, if you must know,' said Edward bluntly, 'we met Lavinia's friend Rose who was most annoying. She proudly introduced us to her gentleman friend but didn't like it when he danced with Lavinia.'

'Really?' said his Mama. 'I thought she was such a quiet little thing.'

'Maybe, but...' began Edward but was interrupted by Lavinia.

'He said I was like a fairy,' she began and then burst out laughing.

'Who's like a fairy?' asked John, just coming into the room.

'Mama,' answered Lavinia with a giggle.

'Mama's like a fairy?' asked a puzzled John.

'That is enough,' said their mother. 'And no wonder Rose was annoyed. You should have handled things better, Lavinia.'

'But what could I have done, Mama?' asked her indignant daughter.

'Throttled him,' grinned Edward. 'Or her,' he added as an afterthought.

'Well, I hope no more is said about it. Now, Lavinia, we have to think about your dress for the ball on Saturday,' said their mother.

'I didn't know…,' began Lavinia, wrinkling her brow.

'I replied to Lady Waverly's invitation. I wonder at your being invited to such a grand ball being so young, but no doubt it will be good experience for you.'

'Yes, Mama,' was all Lavinia said. She turned away, her colour heightened as she remembered Sir Nicholas's words. She didn't know whether to be pleased or sorry that she had promised him the first minuet. If it had been anyone else she would have told her mother but as she was suspicious of Sir Nicholas and knowing his reputation, it was difficult. Lavinia didn't really know whether she favoured him either. First he was horrid to her when she had visited his house with Rose, then he was kind over her unfortunate happening at Lady Brigham's ball and then at the theatre he had been thoughtful again—or had he really? Was he trying to cause her trouble? But at least, his dancing was superior to that of other gentlemen. It should be enjoyable to be his partner but there was always the thought that he might have an ulterior motive in mind.

Her mother called her from upstairs so she hurried to her side to see which dress would be suitable for the ball.

Left alone, and as his Papa and brother were out,

CHAPTER ELEVEN

Edward went to find his favourite book for a quiet read.

'Now look at the dresses you have, Lavinia, and do concentrate, dear. We have to find one suitable as I think it will be an important ball.'

'Why?' asked Lavinia. 'Weren't the others important, then?'

'Yes, of course they were,' answered her Mama testily, 'but I know this address is in a very superior part of London.'

'Well, it doesn't mean Lady Waverly lives there, does it? Many people hire ballrooms...'

'Tut, tut, I don't think so. However, let us look at what we can do with this dress, the pink one which you haven't worn recently. When I went to the shops the other day I bought a length of material, as it was so pretty. See, it has little rosebuds embroidered on it. I thought it could be made into an underskirt, as the pink of the dress is nearly the same colour as the rosebuds. Perhaps a little of the rosebud material could be introduced on the bodice or sleeves somehow to match. What do you think?'

'Oh, yes, it is very pretty. Thank you for buying it for me.'

'Yes, well, I know you will try your hardest to attract a beau but you are leaving it rather late, you know. We have only another two weeks before we return home. Now if I cut the material could you begin to sew, and I'll come and help when I've seen to all the other things I have to do? I believe Selby wanted my opinion on something.'

'Yes, Mama,' said her dutiful daughter, but her heart

wasn't really in the sewing. She knew her parents had tried their best for her so she could marry well. After all, her elder sister had had no trouble but Lavinia had seen or met no one whom she wished to marry. Her parents would be disappointed if nothing came of this London trip but it couldn't be helped and Lavinia supposed that she would have to settle for someone from her home village. She could think of no one suitable at the moment but some stranger might turn up one day. And so her thoughts went on and on while setting small, neat stitches in her altered dress.

All afternoon Lavinia sat in her room and sewed. Was it worth it, she wondered? Her eyes were becoming sore as the daylight inside her room became less and less. But at last the dress was finished as far as Lavinia was concerned. If more needed doing it would have to be left until the morrow. She hung it up. She couldn't even be bothered to try it on to see if it looked pretty. All she wanted was to lie down on her bed and close her eyes.

Half an hour later Mrs Meadows opened the door. 'How are you ...?' She stopped as she saw her daughter curled up upon her bed fast asleep. She looked round and noticed the dress hanging on the hook behind the door. It looked nearly finished so she closed the door quietly and left Lavinia to her slumbers. Anything else that needed doing to the dress would only be small so it could be finished on the next day.

'How do you think we received the invite from Lady Waverly, dear?' Mary Meadows asked her husband. 'After all, we don't know the family.'

Percy looked up from the book he was reading. 'The same way as the other ones, I expect. Names are passed on of eligible girls, aren't they?'

'I suppose so.' But Mary was a little worried as she knew that Lady Waverly was very rich and entertained people of consequence. Perhaps it was those two old ladies who attended every ball who they had to thank for their invitation.

'You will be able to tell us who the people are, dear, which will be interesting,' said Mary with a smile.

'Am I going, then?' Percy looked up from his book, a startled expression on his face.

'But of course, dear. We shall need you.'

Her husband buried his head in his book again, wearing a grieved expression.

The following day, finishing touches were made to the dress and Lavinia tried it on. She was apprehensive but looking in the mirror saw it looked quite pretty with the new underskirt dotted with rosebuds. She smiled rather ruefully as in her mind she would much rather have had a frothy white dress, but that would cost money and her parents had spent plenty of money on her so far. She heaved a sigh. Her mama suggested just a simple band of pink ribbon could be threaded through her hair with perhaps an artificial pink rose over her left ear and she had her mother's white fan as usual, now mended. She felt a little happier now she had tried the dress on; if she couldn't have a new one this was the next best thing. After all, her mother would probably wear her blue gown again.

The evening of the ball arrived and for some reason Lavinia began to feel apprehensive. She knew her dress was pretty and suited her and would have been just right for a friendly ball like the ones where she knew some of the people and those two dear old ladies, but this ball of Lord and Lady Waverly was a different matter. Dignitaries from overseas would be there, and even royalty might be present. Good gracious, would the King be there? She went to find her papa and asked him if he thought this possible.

'Well, I don't really know, of course, but King George is a Hanoverian and from what I hear he spends quite a lot of time in Hanover. Natural, I suppose, if he isn't leading his soldiers into battle somewhere. But we shall see, won't we?' said her father.

Lavinia wasn't comforted. She felt even more apprehensive when they arrived at Lady Waverly's large house. The Meadows's carriage looked plain against some of the splendid coaches which brought beautifully dressed ladies and gentlemen. She could feel her Mama's nervousness but dear Papa just acted as usual, as if he attended such functions regularly. They followed the crowd to the entrance. Everywhere inside was luxurious with highly polished floors and glittering chandeliers. There were also marble pillars and large portraits of elegant people, most likely ancestors. They climbed the stairs following the elite company, the ladies displaying beautiful lace dresses with diamond tiaras and other precious stones. The gentlemen, too, were visions to behold with lace at their throats and wrists over a variety of richly brocaded waistcoats and coats and some younger ones wore high heels. Everywhere was sparkling with colour and light.

At the top of the stairs Mr Meadows gave their names to the major domo who announced them in a stentorian voice and then Lavinia found herself, with her parents, bowing and curtseying to their host and hostess, Lord and Lady Waverly. They looked to be in their mid-forties, very elegantly dressed and in the height of fashion. Lady Waverly was beautiful, Lavinia thought, as she curtsied nervously.

'I am so pleased you could come,' said Lady Waverly. She looked closely at Lavinia and smiled. It was a lovely smile to which Lavinia instantly responded. Lady Waverly nodded and Lavinia followed her parents down the stairs to the large ballroom below, where many people were moving, chatting, laughing and looking for friends. Lavinia wondered where the two old ladies were; she must thank them for suggesting she and her parents were invited.

There were a variety of people, including military gentlemen in their regimentals as well as important parliamentarians. Mr Pitt was present and some of his cronies. They would be soon joined by Lord Waverly, a jolly man by the look of him, when he was relieved from his duty of welcoming guests.

Mr Meadows, with his wife and daughter either side of him, placidly made his way to where some chairs were placed. Some people looked at them with raised brows, others ignored them. This did not bother Lavinia as she was all too busy looking at the colourful scene before her.

'Oh, Mama,' she said, 'doesn't it all look beautiful?'

'Yes, dear, very grand indeed.' It was more than that, thought Mary Meadows. She had never been to such a ball ever and began to be worried how they came to have been invited. She looked round for her husband, who like other older men, were chatting nearby. Why was it that some men could quite happily talk to strangers while it would be unbecoming for ladies to do the same?

Lavinia and her mama watched the dancing and talked to each other. After two dances had been performed, a gavotte and cotillion, the next dance was a minuet and Lavinia suddenly remembered that Sir Nicholas had asked her to dance it with him. Perhaps he hadn't meant it though, she thought, as she looked down at her fingers playing with her fan. She heard her mother say her name. Lavinia looked up expecting to see Sir Nicholas standing there but it was another young man she didn't know. He smiled. 'May I have this dance, dear lady? I'm Rollo Waverly.'

Lavinia didn't know what to do but as her mother was watching she smiled and rose. 'Certainly you may, sir.'

It wasn't until she was being led on to the floor that she saw Sir Nicholas nearby, his face like thunder. She pretended not to notice but quaked inside. How was she to know where he was and more to the point, why hadn't he been a little quicker coming over? She hadn't dared refuse the young man, especially as her mama was there. She tried to forget Sir Nicholas and smiled at her partner. He moved well and she enjoyed dancing with him. She forgot about Sir Nicholas as she turned and glided and moved in the dance.

When it was finished and the final bows and curtsies

were made, Lavinia's partner said how he had enjoyed dancing with her. 'And now I have orders to take you to meet Lady Waverly,' he said.

'Really?' asked a surprised Lavinia. 'Why?'

'I don't know,' he smiled at her. 'She is quite charming, you know. There is no need to worry.'

After carefully wending their way between the other guests thronging the floor, they arrived to where Lady Waverly was sitting on her gold and brocaded couch. Much to Lavinia's surprise she was talking to Sir Nicholas, who was bent over to hear what she was saying. As Lavinia and her partner approached, Lady Waverly looked up and smiled.

'Ah, Rollo, there you are. Miss Meadows, do come and sit by me. And you two,' she instructed Rollo and Sir Nicholas, 'go away.' She waved a hand.

The gentlemen bowed. Sir Nicholas, ignoring Lavinia, said, 'That was a despicable trick to play, Rollo.'

'No, no, I was ordered…' Lavinia heard no more.

'Rollo is my nephew and Nicholas is a friend whom I have known all his life. I knew the family, you know,' said Lady Waverly by way of explaining why she felt able to order him about.

'I see,' said Lavinia. She didn't really see, and why Lady Waverly wanted to speak to her she didn't know either.

'Tell me about yourself and your family. I thought your parents looked very nice,' began Lady Waverly.

'Oh, yes, they are, in fact we are a happy family,' said Lavinia. And as Lady Waverly was looking interested in what she was saying, she continued: 'My sister, who is older than I, is married. Then I'm the next eldest and my brother Edward is sixteen and then there is John who is twelve.'

'So what do they do in London?'

'Edward has fencing lessons and has been to practice dances with me and...'

'But you don't need to practice, my dear. You dance beautifully.'

'Why, thank you, Ma'am,' said Lavinia, blushing.

'So how did you meet Sir Nicholas? You must know I have always known him. His parents were great friends of my husband and I.'

'Were they?' said Lavinia, wondering why they weren't still friends and trying to think what was best to tell her ladyship. 'I met him at Lady Brigham's ball.' And Lavinia went on to tell Lady Waverly how she came to hurt her foot and how Sir Nicholas had taken charge and helped her.

'Now,' said Lady Waverly, when Lavinia had finished, 'you do surprise me. He is not known for his kindness. You're sure it was Sir Nicholas and not someone else who helped you?'

Lavinia smiled. 'No, no, it was indeed Sir Nicholas,' she said.

'So why was he looking at you in a very unkind way just now?'

Good gracious, thought Lavinia, *she doesn't miss anything, does she?* Aloud she said, 'Well, you see, I saw him briefly at the theatre. He enquired after my foot. Then he asked if I was coming to your ball and would I dance the first minuet with him. I said I would but as you saw just now the other gentleman came and I couldn't explain in front of Mama why I couldn't dance with him. Sir Nicholas will either complain or never speak to me again or...'

'Oh dear,' interrupted Lady Waverly, 'that was my fault. Never mind, I will put things right. He is like a son to me, you know. But why do you mind Sir Nicholas's words or looks, Miss Meadows?'

'It's just that I'm not used to someone like him,' was all Lavinia could think of saying.

'I see,' said Lady Waverly and began to talk about fashions and how much she liked Lavinia's pretty dress. But little by little, with gentle questioning, Lady Waverly found out all she wanted to know about the Meadows family.

CHAPTER TWELVE

ONE OF LADY WAVERLY'S servants approached. 'Madam, supper is now ready to be served.'

'Thank you. Tell the musicians, if you please.' The servant bowed and moved away. 'Now let me see,' said Lady Waverly, 'who is there to take you into supper?'

'Oh, that is quite all right. I will find my parents...'

'Ah, just the man,' interrupted Lady Waverly. She raised a hand and Sir Nicholas came over.

'Take this young lady into supper, Nicholas. I've bored her long enough,' she said with a smile.

Sir Nicholas stood before them. 'Your wish is my command, dear lady,' he said, bowing.

'Good,' she said.

So there was nothing for it but for Lavinia to curtsey and turn to Sir Nicholas and place her hand on his arm.

Before Lavinia could say anything, Sir Nicholas asked her if she had enjoyed talking to Lady Waverly.

'Yes, very much. She is very kind, isn't she?'

'I have found her so. And will you dance the next minuet with me, Miss Meadows?'

She glanced up at him. 'As long as you don't glare at me,' she said. 'I really couldn't help...'

'Quietly, Buttercup. I absolve you from what happened. Rollo explained it to me.'

'Oh,' said Lavinia, 'then in that case, yes please.'

'That's better,' grinned Sir Nicholas.

The supper room was large and the food, set out on long tables, looked delicious. To supply such an array for the amount of people invited must have cost something, Lavinia thought.

'Doesn't it all look appetising,' said Lavinia. 'Look at those tiny eggs and the way that beautiful fish has been prepared.'

'Do you think fish beautiful, then?' asked Sir Nicholas with a raised eyebrow.

'Some are very pretty,' Lavinia answered vaguely, but her eyes alighted on the sweetmeats on display.

Her Mama's voice broke in on her thoughts. 'Oh, there you are, and Sir Nicholas, too. Papa has found chairs for us, I see.' And she led the way to a corner where her husband was standing.

Lavinia looked up quickly at Sir Nicholas, in time to catch the glint in his eye. 'Will you please join us, Sir Nicholas?' she said hurriedly, looking anxiously at him.

He looked down at her, seeing her concerned face. 'Thank you. Shall we choose some of this delicious food?' He picked up a tray and between them placed a variety of savouries and sweetmeats onto it. Sir Nicholas carried it back to where Mr and Mrs Meadows were sitting.

Percy immediately stood up. 'Shall we choose some liquid refreshment, too, Sir Nicholas?' he asked.

They came back with three glasses of champagne and one of lemonade.

'Am I not able to have champagne?' Lavinia asked.

'No,' said her Mama forthrightly.

'Perhaps you would care to take a sip of mine, Miss Meadows?' asked Sir Nicholas with a mischievous look in his eye.

'I don't think...' began Mary Meadows.

'A good idea,' said her husband, frowning at her.

Lavinia, smiling mischievously back at him, carefully sipped from the champagne glass Sir Nicholas was holding. He laughed at the look of disgust on her face.

'I'd rather have lemonade, thank you,' she said. 'How you can drink such an odd tasting liquid I don't know.'

Sir Nicholas drank his glass of champagne. 'Enjoy your supper,' was all he said, then, bowing and murmuring their names, he left.

Lavinia felt disappointed as he joined a group of young men and their partners.

'How did you come to be accompanied by that young man, Lavinia?' asked her Mama.

'Lady Waverly asked him to take me down to supper, Mama.'

'Did she? I wonder why? The young man you danced the minuet with looked very pleasant, dear. Does he know Lady Waverly?'

'Yes, he's her nephew. That's why he danced with me— she asked him to and then take me to meet her.'

'Oh, well, that was very nice. And what did you talk about?'

'I told her about my family, briefly, you understand.'

'I see,' said Mary Meadows, not knowing whether to be pleased or sorry.

Everyone began to return to the ballroom. The orchestra started to play once more and couples arranged themselves ready for a cotillion. A young man asked Lavinia to partner him and she was pleased she had refrained from eating too much of the delicious food provided.

Lavinia didn't lack for partners in the dances that followed. It seemed since she had sat and chatted to Lady Waverly she had passed some kind of test and young men didn't hesitate to ask her to partner them. Lavinia began to relax and enjoy herself, which showed by the smiles on her face and her elegant movements. By the time a minuet was announced she looked positively radiant and Sir Nicholas, coming over to where she sat with her parents, found a smiling Lavinia.

'Miss Meadows, may I have this dance?'

'Why thank you sir, I shall be delighted,' she twinkled up at him. Her mama wasn't pleased.

'What have I done to earn your mother's displeasure?' he asked as they took their places.

'I have no idea,' she said, knowing only too well that it was his reputation that her mother objected to. She was pleased that there was no more time for conversation as the music began. The minuet was an elegant and charming dance. After first bowing to each other the partners joined hands, stepping forward then turning to face each other.

Two steps were taken to the right and two to the left with glides. Every step was dainty and danced with dignity and charm. It was really a display of courtship. There was something different in the way Sir Nicholas danced. Every step, every movement was perfect and Lavinia tried to match him. He certainly had a flair for dancing and she enjoyed the experience. His eyes looked on her face as she presented such a pretty picture in her homemade dress. It crossed his mind how wonderful she would look in a more sophisticated gown.

Lavinia, in turn, was fascinated by him and found no difficulty in keeping her eyes on his as the movement of the dance permitted. And as they moved, other couples stopped to watch until eventually they were the only ones dancing on the floor. The music finally finished and the dance ended and Lavinia placed her hand on Sir Nicholas's arm once more. Everyone began to clap. Lavinia, coming out of her dream, looked at her partner who lifted an eyebrow.

'Anything wrong?' he asked.

'Only that I wonder why everyone was watching us,' she said.

'Something to think about when you can't sleep,' he replied.

There was no time for Lavinia to say more as she was returned to her parents. She saw no more of Sir Nicholas that evening and soon afterwards it was time to leave.

On the way home she sat in their cold carriage with rugs placed over her knees. Her father, placid as ever, remarked on the house, the food and the excellence of the champagne and said that after all he had enjoyed himself.

'And the company was very nice too with some very interesting gentlemen to talk to. And Vinny here showing everyone how to dance, it was very well done, dear. Lord and Lady Waverly are very thoughtful people and they came over to see us to chat. And what about you, my dear?' he asked Mary.

'Yes, it was as you say, and Lady Waverly was very kind to speak to us. But I still wonder how she knew of us to invite.'

'I can make a good guess,' remarked her husband, but refused to say more apart from remarking it had been a very pleasant evening.

Lavinia hardly slept the rest of the night. She went over and over again what had happened at the ball. It was true she had felt nervous at the beginning but after she had spoken to Lady Waverly things altered and the minuet she had danced with Sir Nicholas had been wonderful. No other dancer excelled on the dance floor like him; his dancing was sublime. The way he had looked at her as he danced seemed to draw her into his world so that she danced as well as he. It was true he hadn't asked her for another dance but it didn't matter. She went over it all in her mind's eye, the steps, the way Sir Nicholas looked and performed and finally the applause. Eventually in the early hours of the morning she slept.

She was awakened by little Betty drawing the curtains and to the smell of hot chocolate. She groaned as the bright daylight entered the room.

'What time is it?' she murmured sleepily.

'It is half past nine, Miss, and I would have let you carry on sleeping except your mama said I was to wake you. I'll come back when you've drank your hot chocolate, Miss.'

'Thank you,' mumbled Lavinia into her pillow.

The rest of the day was uneventful with Lavinia trying to recover from the previous evening and the boys finding books and games to amuse themselves. They went out as a family for a short walk in a nearby park, which was good, their Papa had said, as there was a wind blowing and it would help to blow the cobwebs away.

The following morning Lavinia and her Mama went to visit Madame Benét for new dresses for them both. Ben drove them in the carriage and then returned to take the gentlemen to their destinations, Edward and John to the fencing academy and their father into the city where his bank was situated. They said they would find their own way home and Ben would collect the ladies at a later hour.

Lavinia was thrilled to be having a new dress. Her others, although pretty, were sadly worn and could only be cut down to trim other dresses or make into some other smaller garment. 'What colour shall we look for, Mama?' she asked, 'and what will you choose?'

'Perhaps a mauve for me and I thought maybe white for you with a touch of pink but we will see what Madame suggests.'

Edward meanwhile presented himself and John at the

fencing academy. John was allowed in to watch and for a time he was interested in what was happening but most of it he had seen before. He wandered and watched others who were further advanced than Edward but after a while even that palled. He decided to wander outside and then he had a very bright thought.

Some time later, his lesson finished, Edward thanked his instructor as usual. His instructor was very pleased with his progress, he said, and told him what to practice for the next lesson. When Edward was ready to leave, he looked for his brother who usually waited for him near the door. Thinking he had stepped outside, he left the building but saw no John. Edward decided to wait for a while thinking that he had become bored and had gone for a walk and would soon return.

The fencing academy was in a quiet area with a path leading to the door either side of which were areas of gravel with some bedraggled plants sitting in tubs, presumably to suggest an idea of luxury. Edward was inspecting these and wondering if he should find water for them when a voice hailed him. 'Hey you!' it called.

Frowning, Edward looked up to behold two dirty and unkempt young individuals of about eighteen years of age, grinning at him. He said nothing.

'It doesn't speak,' said one.

'I wonder if it fights,' said the other.

Edward still said nothing, wondering if he should return to the academy or see if they really meant it.

'Let's see, shall we?' said the first one. Both moved forward together, brandishing swords which had seen better days. They looked to have been found on a rubbish heap somewhere, as they were old and rusty.

Edward automatically drew his sword and stood watching and waiting.

'Oh, look, he wants to fight,' grinned one. Then together they rushed at Edward who, trying to remember what he had been taught, began to fight back. His wrist was supple and he was able to keep them at a distance to begin with but as they moved apart he found it difficult fighting two and he was tired after his lesson, both mentally and physically. However, he tried to concentrate on keeping them in front of him. Then they quickened their pace. Their swordplay was amateurish but they were strong and they began making slashing movements through the air. Edward did his best but he was short of breath, partly through exertion and partly through fright. He thought he heard galloping horses as sweat trickled into his eyes and it was as he tried to blink it away that he felt a searing heat to his upper right arm. His sword fell then and he found himself falling and everything began to go black. His two attackers cheered.

The galloping horses were real enough and they were pulled to a slithering halt. 'Take the reins!' Sir Nicholas shouted to his servant as he jumped down. Dashing to the scene and drawing his sword in readiness, he entered the fray. His first aim was to protect the body on ground and with this in mind he drove back Edward's assailants and moved little by little to stand in front of him. The ruffians had to concentrate hard on warding off Sir Nicholas's lunges, as his aim was deadly accurate, his reach long and his movements like lightning. They did their best to beat him down. But Sir Nicholas thrust and parried so quickly that they didn't know where he was attacking next. With Edward a prostrate form behind him, Sir Nicholas quickened his pace and first one arm of the assailants was slashed and bleeding and then another. The two decided to run for it but Sir Nicholas was quicker. He had no intention of letting them go and he continued his ruthless assault. He had no pity and he soon administered the final thrusts to their hearts and they were no more, apart from two jerking bodies in their death throes, blood seeping from them.

Sir Nicholas gave his blade a quick wipe on one of the bodies and then sheathed his sword and turned to where Edward was lying. Sir Nicholas felt his pulse and discovered it beating. Relieved, he picked up Edward and his sword and carried him to his waiting carriage. He placed him on the seat.

'Drive home as quick as you can, then fetch the surgeon,' he instructed the servant. Meanwhile he whipped off his cravat to staunch the blood now sluggishly seeping through Edward's coat.

When they arrived in Grosvenor Square, Sir Nicholas lifted Edward as best he could and carried him up the steps to his house. As the door opened the carriage was driven off to bring back the doctor. Roberts met him in the hall, gave Sir Nicholas one look and immediately took in the situation. 'Where shall we take him, sir?'

'The room next to mine,' said Sir Nicholas as he began to mount the stairs, still carrying Edward. 'Take his sword and clean it,' he said.

'Yes, of course sir, but I think I had better help you with the young man first. Sword wound, is it?'

'Yes and from ill kept ones.'

Sir Nicholas laid Edward on the bed and looked at him. 'Do we bring him round or...'

'I think it would be best to take his shirt off ready for Doctor Fenwick, sir.'

Between them they stripped Edward and staunched the bleeding on his right arm. 'The wound is deep and I'm worried about the effect of the rusty blades but no doubt Fenwick will have something to stop the poison.'

Soon there was a knock on the door and the doctor was ushered in. Evidently he had wasted no time obeying Sir Nicholas's summons.

'Now, sir, what have you been doing?' he smiled grimly.

'Rescuing this young man from two attackers,' Sir Nicholas replied.

'I see. Let me look at him and bring me some water please.'

For the next half hour the wound was probed and cleaned. Edward began to come round out of his swoon but Doctor Fenwick soon tipped some medicine down his throat, which sent Edward to sleep again. 'He will feel more comfortable when he awakes from that,' he said. 'It won't hurt him to sleep. I don't think any vital spot has been touched. I'll leave you a draught so that if he awakes during the night, as I expect he will, it will help ease the pain. Now I'll stitch the wound and fix a sling for his arm and he can sleep in peace.'

After Doctor Fenwick had left Sir Nicholas told Roberts to organise sitters to stay with Edward. 'He must not be left. If he awakes he will need to be reassured everything is all right. Also see what can be done with his clothes. If there is a problem I am to be called. '

'Do you know him then, sir?' asked Roberts, rather surprised.

'No, not at all. But he fought well and there were two of them.'

'What happened to them, sir?'

Sir Nicholas looked at him disbelievingly. 'What do you think happened to them? Do you think I patted them on their heads and told them to be good in future? I killed them, of course.'

Sir Nicholas went down to his luncheon before meeting a friend that afternoon.

CHAPTER THIRTEEN

'**ARE THE BOYS** back yet?' asked Mary Meadows, passing George and Martin in the hall.

'I haven't see them, ma'am,' they both answered.

'Mm. It's unlike them to be late, they are usually ready for their lunch.' She went in search of her husband whom she found reading the paper he had bought when he went out earlier. 'Are the boys back? Have you seen them, Percy?'

'Mm?' He asked, looking up. 'The boys? No. They'll be along as soon as lunch is on the table, I should think.' And he went on reading.

Mary found her daughter looking out of the window in the morning room. 'Lavinia, have you seen the boys? Luncheon is nearly ready.'

'No, Mama, I haven't seen them. I thought they went out.'

'So they did but they should be back by now.'

'I'll go up to their rooms,' said Lavinia. 'Perhaps they are playing a game with us.'

Her mother issued an impatient sound while Lavinia sped upstairs to find her brothers and warn them to hurry. But when she knocked on each of their doors and looked inside they weren't there. 'So it is obvious,' she said to her mother when she found her downstairs, 'that they are still out.'

They both went to find Percy. 'It is lunch time,' said his wife, 'and the boys aren't back.'

'Well, I suggest we have our lunch, then when they come in they can go and plead with Cook for something to eat,' he said, folding his paper and accompanying them to the dining room. He enjoyed his lunch as usual but Lavinia and her mother were still worried.

'And why are you two not eating?' he asked. 'There are a hundred and one reasons why the boys aren't back. They're growing up. Boys do these kind of things.'

But Lavinia and her Mama weren't happy. By three o'clock there was still no sign of Edward and John. Lavinia persuaded her Papa to go and look for them. In the end he relented and taking George with him in the carriage, which had been brought round, they set forth. Percy thought it best to go to the Fencing Academy first as he could check if Edward had kept his appointment. When they arrived some men were at work on the gravel with buckets of water. As Percy Meadows and George jumped out they asked one of the men what was the trouble

'Oh, sir,' moaned one, 'you should have seen the mess. Blood everywhere.'

'From whom?'

'I don't know who they were, they had been mutilated so much. They were unrecognisable. But they weren't from the Academy, their swords were so decrepit.'

Percy began to feel sick. 'Let's check inside,' he said grimly to George.

They found that Edward had had his lesson as usual and had left. No one could remember John.

'What do we do now?' asked George.

'I think we had better drive around a little and see if we can find them. Perhaps they saw the mess and were upset,' said Percy.

And who could blame them, thought George. Aloud he said: 'You don't think Mr Edward killed them, do you, sir?'

'I don't suppose he'd be strong enough,' said Percy after some thought.

For the next two hours they drove around keeping a sharp look out for Edward and John.

Lavinia was looking out of the window and as soon as she saw the carriage she rushed to the door but when she saw the boys weren't with them she called her mother.

Percy told George not to mention what they had seen at the Academy and just told his wife and daughter that Edward had been for his lesson as usual. They hadn't been seen anywhere after that although they had looked. They would try again later.

'At least they are both together,' said Lavinia, looking on the bright side.

All the rest of the afternoon and evening they listened and waited until Percy Meadows decided to take the carriage once more to see if he could find them. 'If not,' he said, 'I shall have to go to Bow Street tomorrow and see what they can do.'

Later, in Grosvenor Square, Edward became more and more restless. Sir Nicholas was told and he decided it was time for him to take watch over the invalid that night until the morning. 'But sir,' said Roberts, 'I can do that. I am...'

'Yes, I know you are quite capable but it is time you were in bed. You're looking tired. I have spent many nights without sleep, as you probably know. I grant you they were much more fun than this one will be but I shan't sleep on the job.'

'Well, if you're sure, sir, but if you need me...'

'Do you think I'm not capable? Go away,' said Sir Nicholas clinching the matter.

Dressed comfortably in his favourite gown, Sir Nicholas sat at Edward's bedside with the book he had begun reading and an array of lemonade, medicine and a bowl of water and a cloth. He bathed Edward's face, dried it and then lifted him so that he could plump up the pillows and then lay Edward carefully down again.

'My arm,' murmured Edward, 'it hurts.'

'Drink this and it will feel better,' said Sir Nicholas, offering the draught that the doctor had left.

After a sip, Edward moaned. 'Nasty,' he said.

'Maybe,' said his mentor and ruthlessly emptied the remaining contents of the glass down Edward's throat. He coughed and spluttered while Sir Nicholas concentrated on wiping Edward's mouth.

'Go away,' murmured Edward sleepily.

Sir Nicholas grinned. 'Very well,' was all he said.

He stayed where he was though, as Edward slipped back into sleep again. The remainder of the night was uneventful with Sir Nicholas adjusting the bedclothes when Edward became restless.

When Edward awoke next it was daylight. He was aware of a dull ache to his right arm and that he was not in his own bed. No one was with him and he noticed the array of things on the table beside him. He looked round the room, which was lavishly furnished with everything a gentleman might need. The bed and window curtains matched and were in a patterned dark crimson. He could see a pleasing picture on the wall of an outdoor scene in soft greens Everywhere looked expensive but all was in good taste.

All too well did he remember the fight now and wondered what had happened. Evidently he was injured. His right arm throbbed and it was in a sling, so someone had looked after him. He was wondering what he should do when the door opened quietly and Roberts appeared. Seeing Edward was awake he smiled. 'Good morning, do you feel better, sir?'

'Yes, thank you,' said Edward, trying to push himself up in the bed.

'Let me help by placing an extra pillow behind you, sir,' said Roberts.

'But I can get up,' said Edward.

'Not until the doctor has seen you, sir, and then if all is well you will be taken home.'

'I—I see. Thank you. Where am I? I mean, please tell

me, is this your house?'

Roberts smiled. 'No, sir, it belongs to Sir Nicholas Sinclair. Now would you like some breakfast?'

'Good gracious,' said a stunned Edward. Then, pulling himself together he said: 'I'm sorry. I beg your pardon, just—just a drink please.'

'I'll see what I can do, sir,' smiled Roberts and left.

While he waited Edward wondered how it was that he was in Sir Nicholas's house. He must have found him but how and why? And what happened to the two attackers? While Edward was pondering these things the door opened and Roberts appeared carrying a tray on which was a cup of hot chocolate as well as small rounds of bread and butter.

'Here we are, sir,' he said. 'I'll come back in a few minutes when you have finished.'

Edward felt better after his meagre breakfast but he couldn't have taken more; somehow, his appetite for once had failed. He hoped he could soon go home. He knew his family would be worried about him, and what of John? Had he found his way home from wherever it was he had gone?

His breakfast finished, it wasn't long before he heard voices and the door opened. Two gentlemen entered, one quite clearly the doctor, the other presumably Sir Nicholas.

'Sir,' Edward began, but Sir Nicholas interrupted him.

'Oh, you're awake, are you? This is Doctor Fenwick. He is going to check that you and your arm are all right, then you can go home,' said Sir Nicholas.

'Thank you,' said Edward.

The doctor took one look at the wound and pronounced

it was as well as he expected and he didn't poke about as Edward thought he might. He took Edward's pulse and as it was now normal said that there was no need for him to see Edward again until the wound had healed and the stitches could be removed.

'Good,' said Sir Nicholas. 'So, young man, you can get up and I'll take you home.'

While Doctor Fenwick and Sir Nicholas left the room to partake of a glass of sherry, Edward was carefully moving out of bed. Roberts came in to help him dress and then saw him safely downstairs. He awaited Sir Nicholas in the hall where he had sat once before when he had escorted his sister and Rose. Edward felt a little embarrassed as Sir Nicholas had been very kind to him and surely he would remember the Rose incident or at least Lavinia.

'Oh, there you are,' said a voice. 'So what is your name and where are we going?' Sir Nicholas was fastening his cloak as he spoke.

Edward cleared his throat. 'My name is Edward Meadows and the address...' He stopped as Sir Nicholas looked at him.

'Is it, now?' he said slowly, his eyes never leaving Edward's face.

'Yes, sir and the first time I came I—I sat there,' he pointed to the chair.

'It has always puzzled me,' said Sir Nicholas slowly and deliberately, 'why you came at all.'

'Yes, well, it was Rose. She was a kind of friend and her brother said he was meeting you in a duel. Vinny said we would come with her to see you and Rose was to tell you he was under age. But when we came Rose began to panic and cling to me so Vinny said she would see you instead.'

'I see,' said Sir Nicholas.

'Then it turned out,' went on Edward, 'that the brother had dreamt up the whole thing and we needn't have worried. Women!' Edward finished as though he knew all about the gentle sex. Sir Nicholas hid a smile.

'Exactly,' he agreed.

By this time they were about to climb into the carriage that had been brought round and Sir Nicholas suggested Edward gave the driver his address.

It didn't take long before they were in Mount Street.

'Out you get, young man,' said Sir Nicholas. 'Do you need help?'

'But sir, please come in with me. My parents, I am sure, will wish to thank you.'

'I think not, I...'

But the front door had opened and Edward's father had appeared. 'At last, at last you're home,' he said. 'But what happened?' He looked at Edward's arm.

'Papa, here is Sir Nicholas. He has been looking after me. I asked him to come in but...'

'But of course you must come in, dear sir,' said a smiling Mr Meadows.

Sir Nicholas decided it would only take a few minutes to explain everything so he told the coachman to drive round the block.

They went into the morning room where Mrs Meadows was sitting. When she saw her son she went to him, a smile on her face. 'Oh, Edward, thank goodness you are all right—or nearly so,' she added, looking at his arm resting in its sling. 'Come and tell me all about it. Where's John?'

But her husband put an end to her questions. 'Edward has been staying with Sir Nicholas, my dear. He rescued him, evidently, so I insisted he came in to hear his involvement in the matter.'

'Oh, of course,' she said, surprised, and she felt rather dazed at how things were turning out. 'Do be seated, Sir Nicholas, please.'

'Thank you. I have just accompanied Edward home to tell you that the wound isn't life threatening and has been seen by Doctor Fenwick. In another week's time it would be advisable to see him again and perhaps the stitches will be ready to be removed.'

'Thank you, Sir Nicholas, for your help,' said Mary Meadows.

'There was no problem although it concerned me that the wounds were made with dirty swords. But the arm is looking most healthy and there is no need to worry.'

Although Percy Meadows had been busy with the sherry decanter, Sir Nicholas thought it time to leave. He would prefer Edward to tell his own story and not be involved himself. As he was just about to rise, the door burst open and Lavinia rushed in.

'Edward, Edward, you are home!' She ran to him and placed her arms around him, giving him a hug. 'We have been so worried. Are you dreadfully hurt?'

'Lavinia,' said her mother loudly and sharply, 'we have a guest.'

Lavinia looked up and then saw Sir Nicholas. She blushed. 'Sir Nicholas, I beg your pardon, I did not see, I've been so worried…' She swallowed as she knew she was making a mull of things.

Unexpectedly, Sir Nicholas came to her rescue. He had stood up as she had hurried into the room. Surprising himself, he said: 'There is no need to apologise. You must have been very worried about your brother.' He couldn't help it. She looked so pale with dark rings under her eyes as if she hadn't slept.

'Thank you,' she said, looking up at him, 'but what about John? Where is he?'

'I wish I knew,' said Sir Nicholas, really wishing he could just produce him from out of thin air.

'Do not worry Sir Nicholas, Lavinia,' said her mother sharply.

But as she said this there was knocking on the front door. Martin must have opened it as the next moment the door of the morning room was pushed open and a figure burst in. It was black from head to toe. Its clothes were filthy, torn and wet. Its face and hair were black with dirt and mud was all over its shoes and legs. It was John.

Mrs Meadows screamed. His father sat with opened mouth.

But Lavinia ran to him, enfolding him in her arms and giving him a big hug and a kiss on his dirty face.

'Oh, Vinny,' John's hoarse voice shook as he clung to her. 'I tried, I really did.'

'Shush, it's all right now, you're home.' She consoled

him as though he was a much younger child.

'Lavinia, your dress, don't touch him, don't...'

Lavinia ignored her mother and turned. 'Sir Nicholas, I beg your pardon, but please excuse us.' She guided John to the door. Sir Nicholas stood watching them, an expression of surprise and envy on his face.

Mary Meadows broke the spell. 'I suppose I must go and see what is to be done,' she said with a sigh.

'My dear,' said her husband, 'there is no need for you to worry. Lavinia will know what to do and Martin will help.'

'And,' said Edward, 'Vinny will soon find out what he's been doing, although I can guess. But by the time she's finished with him she will have persuaded him what a great adventure he's had and he'll be back to his usual bumptious self.'

Sir Nicholas didn't sit down again. 'Forgive me,' he said. 'I must go. I'm pleased everything has turned out well.' He bowed to Mary Meadows and smiled at Edward as Percy Meadows accompanied him to the door just as his carriage appeared round the corner.

On his way home, Sir Nicholas couldn't forget the picture of a tired and white faced girl rushing to kiss a brother who was filthy and who messed up her dress as he clung to her. He felt a pang of envy and blinked hard to restrain a tear. He hadn't felt like that for a long time. What was happening to him? He decided it would be a good thing to meet up with his friends that evening, preferably for a heavy drinking session.

CHAPTER FOURTEEN

THE FOLLOWING MORNING only Mr and Mrs Meadows sat down to breakfast at the usual time. 'I can understand Edward not joining us,' said his mother, 'as he is probably in pain, but John and Lavinia should be here, don't you think, dear?'

'Well, I don't know,' said her husband, not wanting to argue with her but not really agreeing with her either, 'from what John said he didn't sleep much before and Lavinia hasn't slept well for worrying about them both.'

'Mm,' mused his wife, eating her usual bread and butter. 'I wonder what John really did? Vinny said he was so tired he didn't tell her much. He ate then went to bed. He was fast asleep when I looked at him later, but at least he was clean.'

Percy laughed. 'He certainly looked a sight when he came in. Don't be too hard on him, dear.'

'I hope Vinny comes soon as we are supposed to see Madame Benét about her new dress. I'm afraid this trip to London hasn't been as successful as we thought. Vinny hasn't met anyone she likes, we shall have to pay the doctor's bill for Edward, and it will be expensive if he attends Sir Nicholas, and John will have to have new clothes as those he was wearing will have to be thrown away. We shall have to stay a little longer and...'

'But my dear,' said her husband, tired of her moaning, 'we already said we would stay another week or two so let us say no more.'

The door opened and Lavinia came in. 'Good morning Papa, Mama. I'm sorry I'm late. I overslept and I should have gone on sleeping if Betty hadn't awoken me.'

'There's some breakfast left, I think,' said her father with a smile.

'Isn't it good to have the boys back again? John went to dig in the mud by the Thames, you know. He said he thoroughly enjoyed himself and he found some pieces of jewellery, which he will show you. He said he didn't realise the time had gone so quickly and it became dark as he tried to find his way back home so he became completely lost in the streets. Then it rained and he sheltered in doorways through the night but when it became light he managed to find someone who told him the way. He said he hardly slept and he hadn't had anything to eat and he was starving.'

'Typical John,' said his father. 'But we'll see what he says when he eventually comes down.'

'But please don't be vexed with him. He was very frightened, you know,' said Lavinia.

'I wonder what Sir Nicholas thought,' said Mary Meadows. 'He always makes me feel uncomfortable.'

'I think he did just as he ought,' said her husband. 'And Edward owes his life to him, you know.'

'Oh? How is that, then?' asked Mary.

'When I went looking for Edward I began with the Fencing Academy and found some men cleaning up a great mess outside where fighting had taken place. I cannot go into details but I fancy if Sir Nicholas hadn't been there, and how he came to be there I don't know, our Edward would be no more.'

'Oh, dear, I didn't know,' said Mary. 'Thank goodness Edward can't go there anymore. No one is safe these days, are they? I shall be pleased when we can go home. At least we know most people there and we can feel safe.'

No more was said as the three of them ate their breakfast. They were concerned only with their own thoughts.

It was broken by Edward opening the door. 'Good morning everyone,' he said.

'How are you, Edward?' asked Lavinia. 'Did you sleep all right?'

'Not too bad. I took the pills the doctor gave me and they helped. It's awkward as I can't turn over properly.'

'Never mind, dear,' said his Mama. 'Take it easy for a day or two.'

'What happened though, Edward?' asked Lavinia.

'Oh, after my fencing lesson, I came out of the door hoping to find John but two ruffians attacked me with swords. I tried to keep them away from me but there were two and I found I couldn't look at both at once. Then one struck me. It all went black and I woke up in a room in Sir Nicholas's house yesterday morning.'

'When you've had the stitches out it will feel easier, I expect,' said his father. 'Can you manage to eat with your left hand? Can I cut anything up for you?'

'Now, Lavinia,' said her Mama, turning to her daughter, 'we have a busy day. This morning we must go and see about our new dresses and if they are finished we can wear them tonight. This afternoon we go to Mrs Carson's to take tea with her and her friends, you know.'

'Yes, Mama,' said Lavinia, feeling she would rather sleep. 'Where do we go this evening?'

'Why, to Lady Gilmore's. She very kindly invited us. You can't have forgotten, surely? I expect you will see some friends, you know, and...'

'Yes, Mama,' was all Lavinia could think to say. She hoped by the time the evening came she would have more energy.

They were interrupted once more, this time by John who opened the door and strode in. 'Have I missed breakfast?' he asked. He was dressed as though in a hurry as indeed he had been, having woken up with a gnawing feeling in his stomach.

'John, I thought you'd sleep later,' said his mother.

'Well, I might be tired later on but I'm hungry. I missed some meals yesterday, you know.' He sat down waiting for a plate of cold meat to be served to him. 'Would you like to see what I found yesterday on the edge of the river?'

'Yes please,' said Lavinia.

'Not at the breakfast table,' said his mother.

'They are clean, Mama. I have washed them.' From his pocket he took out a ring, a brooch, a chain and a piece of gold.

'How wonderful,' said Lavinia.

'The gold piece looks as though it was the back of something, I think, perhaps a snuff box. The ring has a small stone, possibly a diamond set in the gold and the brooch would have been very pretty when it was new. It's of a bird with some precious stones but a few of the smaller stones are missing. The chain could be gold, I suppose, I don't really know.'

'How interesting,' said his Papa, 'now what will you do with them? Keep them?'

'I don't know yet. I haven't thought about it,' said John.

'You could take them to a jewellers and see how much they are worth,' suggested Edward. 'Then you can decide whether to keep them or not.'

'This is all very interesting,' said their Mama, 'but come along, Lavinia, we must visit the dressmaker.'

'Yes, Mama,' said her daughter.

They duly set off taking the carriage. It was a sunny day, which cheered Lavinia up a little, but she didn't really feel like trying on her new dress. But perhaps when she saw it she would think differently, she hoped.

Madame Benét was waiting for them and so were the dresses. The white lace dress looked pretty, Lavinia thought, with fine lace at the elbows and an under gown of pink satin. It was cut low across the bosom, which her Mama thought indecorous, but when Lavinia tried it on Madame Benét inserted some ruched lace, which pleased Mrs Meadows. Her own dress was of mauve silk and looked very elegant. Both ladies were pleased and while Mrs Meadows paid, the dresses were boxed and taken out to the carriage.

'We will go back home now and you can rest a little before lunch,' she said to Lavinia. 'You look decidedly jaded, dear. Ask Betty to hang up your blue dress for this afternoon. It will be just right for tea at Mrs Carson's. Also this new dress must be hung too. If you are still pale this evening we shall have to apply a little rouge, won't we?' And so her Mama continued while Lavinia answered just 'yes' or 'no' or nothing at all. She thought it must be her Mama's reaction to having the boys back home again after being so worried about them.

The afternoon at Mrs Carson's was pleasant but would have been better for Lavinia if she felt less tired. The young people that were there were friendly but there was no one whom Lavinia wished to see again. She took part in their conversations but on the way home felt, somehow, it had been a waste of time. The girls had been younger than Lavinia and the young men either thought too much of themselves or were shy. However, Lavinia was able to rest for a couple of hours before they were due at Lady Gilmore's and when Betty awoke her she felt a little better. She was able to appreciate her new dress a little more and Selby came in to dress her hair and she swept her curls to the side with pink ribbon and placed some pink rosebuds above her ear. She gave Lavinia her fan, which was still broken. She had tried to mend it, but to no avail, so she just carried it. Lavinia didn't like to ask for a new one, as she knew her mother wasn't pleased with her as she had had such high hopes of Lavinia's forthcoming nuptials. She donned her cloak and went downstairs to join her parents, who were waiting. The boys were going to have a quiet evening reading or perhaps playing chess or card games, they said, and their father told them both to have an early night.

Lady Gilmore's house was in a fashionable part of London. She was one of the elite few who prided herself on engaging the best orchestra and the best dancers, and giving the most delectable suppers. Whether others agreed with this or not didn't matter, as she always had a good response to her invitations and, of course, the two ladies who always attended were Effie and Dru. This particular evening they each sat in comfortable chairs placed together in a strategic position near the wall, halfway down the room so that they could see and hear whatever was going on. Dru wore a silk dress in old gold with a heavy gold chain on which hung an emerald. Effie wore dark blue and diamonds.

'Of course,' Dru was saying, 'lots of people we know were invited to Lady Waverly's ball, weren't they?'

'Yes, dear, but you know her balls are really for parliamentarians and the military. You know, the important people of the country. It keeps her husband happy, I believe,' said Effie.

'I know,' said Dru, 'but I heard that the Meadows girl and her parents were invited, which seems unusual. But she excelled herself in dancing with you know who,' she nodded wisely.

'Sir Nick, you mean, dear?' asked Dru.

Effie nodded. 'I wonder if they both will be here

tonight?'

They gazed around at everyone who had been invited; all seemed to be dressed beautifully. The ballroom was pretty too, with drapes of gold and blue, large arrangements of flowers and the chandeliers sparkling above. The gentlemen of the orchestra had arrived and quickly sat down and arranged their music.

'Look, Eff, there's the little Meadows girl with her parents, I think.'

'Where, dear?' asked Dru, craning her neck to see. 'Oh, yes, she is curtseying to Lady Gilmore. Oh, they are coming past. Smile, dear.'

Lavinia saw the ladies and went up to them and curtsied. 'Good evening,' she said. 'How nice to see you again. How are you?'

Effie and Dru smiled back at her. 'How kind of you to ask,' they said.

'We are well and hope to see you dance, Miss Meadows,' said Dru.

'I hope your ankle is better,' said Effie.

'Thank you, yes. Excuse me.' Lavinia curtsied and went to join her parents who stood waiting for her. They nodded at the ladies and moved on.

'She is a sweet girl,' said Effie, 'but I thought she looked tired. What do you think, dear?'

'Maybe, maybe,' said Dru. 'She is wearing a new dress which is pretty but white is not the colour to wear when you're tired.'

'I wonder why they came, then? But I suppose if they

had accepted the invitation they had to come.'

'More likely,' said Effie knowingly, 'the dear girl hasn't found a beau to propose to her and time is running out.'

'Oh dear, I hope that's not the case. She is such a sweet little thing. Let us watch and see.'

Ten minutes later of watching guests arrive, Effie dug Dru in the ribs with a fat elbow. 'Look, Dru,' she said, nodding towards the entrance.

Sir Nicholas had arrived.

He stood there, looking elegant, handsome and self assured as usual, in a coat of darkest maroon trimmed with silver. His waistcoat was of black figured silk, above which the finest lace showed at his throat. He bowed over Lady Gilmore's hand as she welcomed him with a smile.

'Well, Sir Nicholas, how nice to see you after such a long time.'

'I know, dear lady, but I always look forward to your balls even if I cannot always attend them. I hope I may have the honour of the first dance with you tonight?'

'Only if it is a slow one. At my age, you understand…'

'I don't really understand what you are saying, but if it is a slow dance you wish for, a slow dance it shall be.' He bowed and quickly made his way to the orchestra. After a few words, they nodded and began to play music for a stately minuet. Sir Nicholas claimed his hostess's hand and the ball had begun.

Lavinia had noticed the entrance of Sir Nicholas and wondered if he would ask her to dance. She didn't know whether she wished him to or not. If she did dance with him she would have to be alert so as not to disgrace either of them. The music helped to make Lavinia feel livelier but for all that she wished she hadn't come. Her mama looked lovely in her new mauve dress with its lace and her amethyst earrings, thought Lavinia, and no doubt she was enjoying it and doing her best to support her daughter in her search for a husband, which made Lavinia feel even worse. She would liked to have fanned herself but she reminded herself that she only carried the fan for show as it was broken—and she was the one who had broken it. So instead of chatting and smiling and looking the picture of a pretty girl, Lavinia looked pale, worried and serious.

As the minuet was coming to an end Sir Nicholas glanced round the room and noticed Lavinia sitting quietly with her mama. He could see there was something wrong and thought he must find out as the poor girl looked ill. After he had returned Lady Gilmore to her friends he carefully looked among the gentlemen and saw Mr Meadows with his acquaintances. Sir Nicholas quickly moved towards him. He bowed. 'Gentlemen, forgive the interruption but may I have a word with you, Mr Meadows?'

'Certainly.'

'It is just,' said Sir Nicholas quietly, 'that I see your daughter looking far from well. May I have your permission to take her on to the terrace for some fresh air, and I will procure her a drink. I promise I will look after her as I should.' His eyes were serious as he looked at Percy Meadows, who nodded.

'Very well, I should have noticed. I will take you over to

her. Perhaps she will feel better with a little attention.'

And so a few minutes later Lavinia and her mother were surprised to see her Papa with Sir Nicholas.

'Lavinia, Sir Nicholas has asked permission to take you for some refreshment if you care to go with him.'

Lavinia looked up quickly. 'Oh, yes. How kind,' she murmured, unsure what she should do.

Percy Meadows was talking to his wife. 'There is no need for you to worry, my dear. Sir Nicholas has promised to look after her.'

And so, as if in a dream, Lavinia walked away with her hand on Sir Nicholas's arm. He led her to the terrace, asking her what she would like to drink.

'I think it had better be lemonade, please,' she said with a smile.

'Could you bring lemonade for the lady and wine for me, please?' He passed a coin into the lackey's hand.

'Of course, sir,' he bowed and moved away.

'Come and sit down on the seat, Miss Meadows.' He stood while she sat down and then sat beside her, but not too close.

'So why are you looking pale and wan? It's not like you, you know. Are you ill?'

This did produce a smile. 'No, of course not. It is just that I am very tired. I did my best to rest when I could so that I should be well for this evening but I really need to sleep, I think. I'm sorry, I...'

'There's no need to be. Your brothers are recovered, more or less, I hope?'

'Oh yes. John is nearly back to his usual self and Edward will be better after the stitches are out. He goes to the Doctor soon, I believe.'

'Good, and then you can stop worrying about them.'

'Well, it's natural to worry about those you love, isn't it?' said Lavinia.

'Yes, of course,' said Sir Nicholas, wondering if that was true.

The lackey returned and placed the tray with the drinks on a small table, which he moved towards the seat. He bowed, saying, 'If you require anything else, sir, I am not far away.'

'Thank you,' said Sir Nicholas with a nod.

He handed Lavinia her drink and picked up his glass of wine. 'Tell me,' he said, 'why are you here tonight if you do not feel well enough?'

'Because I'm not ill, just tired. We had new dresses made and accepted the invitation so we couldn't...'

'You could. Is it because your Mama wants you to find a young man to marry?'

'Well, yes, that is why we came to London, like anyone else and...'

'And?' he asked as she paused.

'I—I've been a disappointment to my parents.' Her voice faltered and she looked down into her glass of lemonade.

There was a pause until Sir Nicholas said with a smile, 'You are supposed to drink it, not look for answers in it. Would you prefer this wine?'

Lavinia looked up with a little smile. 'No, oh no,' she said.

'That's better,' said Sir Nicholas.

Lady Gilmore appeared. 'Forgive me, but is everything all right?' she asked.

Sir Nicholas looked at Lavinia. 'Oh, yes, yes, of course,' she said. 'I'm just a little tired, that is all and Sir Nicholas procured a drink for me.'

'Oh, good, so just rest awhile,' smiled Lady Gilmore, and withdrew. She had noticed Mrs Meadows becoming anxious and so had come to see. Now she trod over to her. 'There is no need to worry. Lavinia is sipping lemonade and they are just chatting.'

At the moment Sir Nicholas was asking Lavinia a question. 'Miss Meadows, are you frightened of me?'

Lavinia looked at him quickly. 'Frightened of you? No, I don't think so. Why?'

He flicked her cheek with a finger and smiled. 'Good girl,' he said. 'We had better return to the ballroom. Do you think you could dance with me now?'

Lavinia nodded and smiled, looking up at him. 'I can try,' she said.

CHAPTER FIFTEEN

SIR NICHOLAS reached home in a happy state of mind that night. He had had a delightful evening. He jumped down, thanked the coachman and climbed up the steps as the door was opened, not by the usual footman, but by Roberts himself.

Sir Nicholas frowned. 'Why have you waited up for me? You should be abed.'

Roberts closed the door. 'I sent the footman to bed as I wished to speak to you about a visitor, sir.'

Sir Nicholas frowned. 'A visitor? Who is it?'

'It is Mr Bradley, sir. He has come all the way from Surrey today to see you about Sinclair House. He was very tired so I suggested he went to bed after a light meal, as he's not so young as he used to be, sir. I said you would see him in the morning.'

'Do you know what it is all about?' asked Sir Nicholas, not too pleased at the news.

'No, sir, but he did say it was urgent and that was why he came in person.'

'I see. Go to bed, Roberts. I'll see him in the morning then, thank you.' Frowning, he climbed the stairs to his own room.

It was long before he drifted off to sleep as part of his

brain still dwelt on the sweet face of Lavinia and another part wondered what could have happened to his house in Surrey to make Bradley come all the way to see him. Eventually, worn out with thinking, he slept.

Although his night had been disturbed Sir Nicholas was up at the usual time. He said he would breakfast as soon as Mr Bradley appeared and went off to look at his horses and tell the coachman to be ready for a long journey if needs be. When he had finished he returned to the house to find Mr Bradley awaiting him and his breakfast.

After the initial welcome they sat down and talked while they ate. Mr Bradley was a gentleman in his sixties with a pleasant voice and a gentle demeanour. He had been looking after Sinclair House before Sir Nicholas was born.

'So Mr Bradley, what brings you all this way to see me? Nothing too horrendous, I hope?'

'Well, it is a while since you visited, sir, and I quite understand why, but certain things need doing which I think you should know about as they will cost money.' And he went on to enumerate the problems, some simple like decorating most of the rooms, others structural like outside pillars needing replacing.

'I see. And the staff?'

'They are still the same apart from the one or two of the older ones retiring who you knew about. We have taken on some younger staff as well. They all work well but it would be good if you visited from time to time, sir.'

'Mm,' said Sir Nicholas. He really didn't wish to leave London just at this present time. But on the other hand he suspected Mr Bradley wouldn't come himself if it wasn't very important. 'So do you wish me to return with you?'

Mr Bradley's face lit up. 'Sir Nicholas, it would be wonderful if you would and we could go through the house outside and in and make it as it should be again.'

'Mmm.' Sir Nicholas didn't seem so enthusiastic but the house belonged to him now, he thought, and he ought not to let it go to rack and ruin. It was the memories that had stopped him visiting, not that he didn't like the house. His engagements he could easily forget about and you never knew, perhaps one day in the distant future, he might take his bride there as his father had done before him.

'And are you well enough to travel today, Mr Bradley?' asked Sir Nicholas with a smile.

'Yes, sir, of course.' Poor Mr Bradley hoped he was well enough. He would have liked a day or two to rest, really, but if Sir Nicholas wanted to go today he wouldn't say no. He thought he would have had a more difficult time trying to persuade him to set forth and wondered why very little persuasion had been needed. This was a good day, indeed.

So Sir Nicholas set forth later in the day to visit his old home, hoping he would soon be back again in London.

Mr Bradley was pleased to be invited to travel with Sir Nicholas in his coach and hoped that he would feel better for a quicker journey.

Lavinia went to bed that night after Lady Gilmore's ball in a confused state of mind. She had danced with Sir Nicholas and he had been supportive, taking her hand before she offered it or turning her round in case she forgot. He really had helped her not to look stupid or disgrace him. She had thanked him for his help at the end as he led her back to Mama, but he had just smiled at her and murmured 'Poor little Buttercup.' Did she like him now? He had asked if she was still frightened of him and she had answered honestly. He didn't frighten her but he puzzled her. Did he really like her and would he come calling or was he just amusing himself? Perhaps the following day would give the answer when she hoped he would call and be concerned for her health. She hugged herself with the pleasure to come and finally slept.

The next morning Mary Meadows was still pleased to receive invitations, which extended to her daughter, to various forms of entertainment from balls and musical evenings, to a trip to Vauxhall Gardens from Mr and Mrs Gilbert for all the family on the following Wednesday. This latter invite suited Mary very well as it would be their last week in London and the last outing before returning home, and if Edward was well enough, which she hoped would be the case, it would be a fitting final entertainment for them all. Some balls and entertainments would have to be refused, regrettably, as they would have returned home by then. Mary sighed. She supposed Lavinia had done her best and it was no use being annoyed with her. It was a pity she had had the misfortune to meet Sir Nicholas Sinclair as he was so very attractive, but those kind of men and their lifestyle didn't make for good husbands. It was a pity he had crossed their paths but, of course, in Edward's case it had been a very good thing. And so the thoughts went round and round in her brain as she busied herself around the house.

Lavinia came in to see if her mother had made any plans for the day. Mary hadn't but showed her the invitations that they could attend during their final week. 'And there is a ball tomorrow night which will be our last large affair, Vinny,' she said.

'That's nice,' said her daughter, wondering if Sir Nicholas would be there but not saying anything. 'I must look at my dresses then.'

'And we are going, all being well, to meet the Gilberts in Vauxhall Gardens next week, which will be our last trip. So all of us can go, as I'm sure the boys will like to walk around the gardens too. Now, today we have time to check our dresses and see if they are fit to be seen and perhaps we can have a gentle walk in the park as a family for a change.'

Lavinia hoped if Sir Nicholas was going to visit that he would come soon.

But as the morning progressed it seemed less likely and then lunchtime came and Lavinia felt let down and was disappointed.

The following day Percy took his son to visit the doctor. They found him very kind and professional and after looking at Edward's arm said he was sure everything would be perfect after the stitches were out. It wasn't quite such an ordeal as Edward had expected and he was told to take care how he dressed himself and everything should be all right. When his father thanked the doctor and asked him what he owed him, the doctor said that Sir Nicholas had already paid for the treatment from the start and therefore there was no more to pay.

'What shall we do?' asked Edward when they left.

'We can go and call on Sir Nicholas and offer to pay him. I'm sure he won't accept anything but we must offer.'

'Yes, he was very kind to me,' said Edward, nodding. He gave the driver the address and soon they were in Grosvenor Square. They asked to see Sir Nicholas and the lackey invited them inside. In a few moments Roberts came towards them. 'Why Mr Edward, how are you?' he asked, smiling.

'Good morning, Mr Roberts. This is my father. I am very well now, thank you and we have just come from Doctor Fenwick's.'

'We wished to see Sir Nicholas as there seems to be some mistake. He has paid for my son's treatment and I wished to make things right with him.'

'I see, sir,' said Roberts. 'I'm sure Sir Nicholas wouldn't wish you to reimburse him and unfortunately we cannot ask him as he has gone into Surrey this morning and we don't know when he'll return.'

'Oh, I see,' said Mr Meadows. 'When you do see him will you please thank him and tell him we called?'

'Of course, sir,' bowed Roberts.

Mary Meadows had mixed feelings when her husband told her about Sir Nicholas. 'I'm sure it is very kind of him to pay the doctor but I suppose to him it isn't such a big thing as he is very wealthy.'

'If what people say is true,' her husband nodded. 'But I would still have liked to have thanked him, at least. I might never see him again as he has gone into Surrey.'

'Why Surrey, I wonder,' said Edward.

'Perhaps he has friends there,' said his father.

Lavinia, having just come into the room, heard some of these comments. 'Who has gone into Surrey?' she asked.

Edward grinned. 'Why, Sir Nicholas. I expect he's tired of all these balls and people and has gone to friends for a bit of peace. I know if I were in his shoes I'd do the same. It is much nicer to be in the fresh air than cooped up in smelly London. I know I shall be pleased to be home next week.'

Lavinia didn't say anything. She was shocked. If he had gone away at such short notice, was it her fault? Had she said or done something that he hadn't liked? Who was he visiting there? During the rest of the day she did as she should but all the time something in her brain nagged her. Why had he gone? Was she expecting more from him than he intended to give? Had he just been flirting with her?

However when she was ready that evening for the last ball she would attend in London she tried to put him out of her mind and think only of enjoying herself.

To a certain extent Lavinia was successful. She knew her parents kept an eye on her so she was careful not to overdo the gaiety, which she was far from feeling. However, she must have succeeded in looking pleased with everything, as she never lacked for a partner. They were young, pleasant and danced well so Lavinia didn't have any complaints to make but they just weren't Sir Nicholas. Mrs Meadows watched carefully and gave her daughter and her various partners smiles of encouragement.

Two other ladies who gave Lavinia smiles were Effie and Dru. 'A pretty little thing but it's a shame she hasn't been successful in finding a husband. I expect her mother is disappointed,' said Dru.

'Mm,' said Effie. 'You know, I think she and Sir Nicholas would suit each other. They both dance well and she is pretty and he is handsome. She would give him a good run for his money, too. She has spirit.'

'Where is Sir Nicholas tonight, I wonder?'

Effie shrugged. 'Perhaps he wasn't invited,' she said.

'Oh, Effie, not invite Sir Nicholas? Everyone invites him.'

'Well,' said Effie, 'let's say then he didn't choose to accept.'

The dance ended and as Lavinia and her partner passed by, the two ladies waved to her.

'Oh,' said Lavinia, 'excuse me, I must speak to the ladies.'

Her partner bowed and moved away.

'How are you, ladies?' Lavinia sat down on a stool placed conveniently near. 'I'm pleased I have seen you,' she went on, 'as this is my last ball in London as we have to go home next week.'

'Oh dear,' said Dru, 'how sad. We shall miss you, dear.'

'Thank you. I shall miss you too,' Lavinia replied dutifully.

'Where is your home, dear? Is it far away?' asked Effie.

'It is a small but pretty place called Limwood and it is in Kent, just, I think. We have a house there which is the largest in the village but not as large as some of the London houses. We have a small terraced garden and a little wood too which was good for playing in when we were children.'

'It sounds very nice, dear, doesn't it, Eff?' said Dru.

'The villagers are happy people, I think, and there are some charming little shops,' went on Lavinia, trying to give them a good impression of her home.

'I don't suppose you have heard where Sir Nicholas is, have you, dear? He usually attends the balls we do and we miss him,' said Effie.

'My father said he had gone into Surrey but that is all I know.' Lavinia stood up. 'I must go back to Mama. It has been lovely meeting you, ladies. Goodbye.' She gave them a smile and a curtsey but the ladies were quick to see that the smile broke in the middle as she hurried away.

Then Lavinia saw M de Craon. He was back again. She had begun to think he had left London, as he hadn't been present at other dances Lavinia had attended. She hoped he wouldn't ask her to dance. But when Lavinia returned to her parents he followed her. He bowed. 'Miss Meadows, may I have the next dance? I promise not to tread on you,' he smiled.

Lavinia felt her smile was forced and not spontaneous. She didn't want to dance with him; she really wished she knew what to say, but with her mama sitting next to her how could she refuse him?

Her mother was now interrupting. 'Monsieur de Craon,

how nice to see you again. Have you been away? We missed you.'

M de Craon looked surprised but managed a smile. 'I am flattered you noticed my absence, Madame,' he bowed.

Mrs Meadows looked at her daughter. 'I'm sure Lavinia would love to dance the quadrille with you,' she said, looking pointedly at Lavinia, who sighed to herself but dutifully murmured, 'Thank you, Monsieur.'

CHAPTER SIXTEEN

IT WAS the Wednesday morning when the Meadows family had accepted the invitation to meet the Gilbert family at Vauxhall Gardens. The day after, they were going home. They all had been busy packing so that there was nothing left to do and they could enjoy this last day in London. Mrs Meadows felt a little tired and disappointed as she had been sure Lavinia would have met her future husband at one of the assemblies as her older sister had done before her. Lavinia's Papa, on the other hand, didn't seem at all perturbed about the fact, saying that Lavinia was perhaps too young. When his wife pointed out to him that his elder daughter had been the same age as Lavinia was now, he had shrugged his shoulders and said: 'She's different.' His wife had dismissed the remark with a decided 'Tcha'.

Edward and John were looking forward to being out in the air and hoped the gardens would be interesting, perhaps with some fountains. A game of hide and seek might be possible, they thought. And Lavinia, recovered from her tiredness, looked forward to meeting Sophy again. If she could chat to her for a while, perhaps she wouldn't feel so bad about returning home in disgrace, for she felt she had disappointed them all, especially her mother.

They were all ready and after Mary Meadows looked at

her children to see if they were neat and tidy and the boys had clean shoes, they trod down the steps to where Ben was waiting with the carriage. They were a little squashed, the boys complaining loudly, but as their father told them, they could stretch their legs for as long as they liked afterwards when they had arrived at the gardens. Their mother said that as a matter of fact, if they all sat still there would be nothing to worry about.

Percy Meadows took a small guidebook from his pocket and said they would soon be crossing Westminster Bridge, so there was the River Thames to look at and the craft which plied their trade. Also, he added, quoting from his book, '"the bridge was built by a Swiss gentleman by the name of Labelye between the years of 1739 and 1750. It is 1038 feet long and 44 feet wide."'

'Good gracious,' said his wife, 'it is nearly new. Only a few years old. I do hope it is safe. Perhaps we should have travelled by boat, after all.'

'How does anyone build a bridge over water?' enquired John. 'I mean, how do they get it to stay up?'

'Well,' said his father, 'I don't really know. It has sorts of pillars underneath which go into the ground. But how they do it I've no idea. I'm not a bridge builder.'

'He must be very clever,' said Edward.

'It feels as though it is swaying,' said his mother, her face losing a little colour.

'Well, I think we're safe enough, dear. Other carriages are going over too, you know. It is not just us. We should be safe enough,' said her husband calmly. And to try and take her mind off the bridge he read out about the gardens.

"'Some years before the present date,'" he read aloud, "'the gardens were all redesigned as originally they had been a landscaped public garden. Now they have fountains, artificial ruins and gravel paths on which to walk.'"

A good place to explore, thought the boys. Their eyes were on the river, watching the different craft there as their carriage went over the bridge and then followed the road until they came to the main gate of Vauxhall Gardens.

They were all glad to alight, as the day was warm and the temperature inside the carriage with five people was uncomfortable. Percy Meadows wished he wore a smaller wig. Perhaps on the return journey he and the boys could cross the Thames by boat and meet the carriage the other side.

They came to the main gate and waiting for them was Mr Gilbert who greeted them all warmly. They all walked up a gravel path to where Mrs Gilbert, Sophy and her brothers were sitting. As soon as they saw the Meadows family approaching they stood and came to greet them. They decided to walk towards the centre of the gardens. Sophy soon renewed her friendship with Lavinia.

They walked between the flower beds and admired them, Mrs Gilbert especially, as she liked her flower garden at home and worked on it herself, apart from the digging, of course. Edward and John were pleased to meet the Gilbert boys again and they all were given permission to go off on their own to explore the first 'ruin' they saw. The gentlemen discussed the state of the country and what they would do if they sat in parliament. Sophy, of course, soon told Lavinia how much she missed Martin as he had gone away with his family and Lavinia told Sophy about her failure to find a husband.

'But Lavinia, if you haven't met anyone suitable you're not to be blamed for that, surely.'

'Well, Mama is disappointed in me. You see, my elder sister was so lucky to find her husband. He is such a dear, too, so of course Mama expected me to do the same.'

'I suppose I'm lucky, then,' said Sophy. 'My sister and brothers are older than I am and, of course, they are married. I am the last to leave and I think Mama will miss having her family, or part of it. But what about that young man at the theatre? The one who visited you in the box. He was very handsome, I thought.'

'Yes, well,' said Lavinia, looking down at her fingers, 'Mama doesn't approve of him and indeed I cannot blame her.'

'Why?' asked Sophy. 'Do tell me.'

'Well,' said Lavinia with a little smile, 'he is well known for the type of company he keeps—women, you know,' she whispered. 'But he is a brilliant swordsman and will kill anyone.' She went on to describe what happened to Edward. 'And his dancing is out of this world, too,' she finished dreamily.

'I think you like him, don't you?' asked Sophy with a smile.

Lavinia nodded. 'I think I do but he isn't bothered about me as he seems suddenly to have left London. So...' She shrugged her shoulders and spread her hands.

'Oh, dear,' sighed Sophy, 'we are a pair, aren't we? Oh look, our Mamas are sitting on a seat. Let us find one and do the same. Where are the boys, I wonder?'

Edward and John had found another ruin to explore. 'Are you pleased to be going home, John?' asked Edward.

'Yes, it is all so smelly in London with large buildings and the streets are full of people and coaches. It was fun finding my treasure. But I'm pleased we are going home. Do you think we shall have to do it all over again if Vinny doesn't find a husband? I mean, come back to London?'

'I don't know. It's been quite an expensive trip, I believe. I shall be pleased to go home too. I still have nightmares about being attacked by those men. I am lucky to be alive. Yes, I shall be pleased to go home.'

The gentlemen had discovered an area where tables and chairs were set out so that visitors could partake of refreshments. They ushered their respective families to sit down and they found chairs in the shade of the trees where they chatted and watched the world go by.

The men discussed the affairs of the day, the ladies talked of fashions and the girls wondered how long it would be before they married. The boys sat looking at the view before them of trees, flowers and a playful dog and discussed what they would do when they returned home.

Mrs Gilbert, noticing that the girls had become friendly with each other, as proved by their continual chat and giggles, turned to Mrs Meadows. 'Look how those two are enjoying themselves. I don't think they have stopped talking all the time they've been here.'

'Yes, they are both sweet girls and I suppose they find they have a lot in common,' said Mrs Meadows.

'I wonder,' said Mrs Gilbert, thoughtfully, 'if you would consider Lavinia coming to stay with us for a few days. Sophy's friend has had to go away with his parents, you know. I'm sure she would love Lavinia's company.'

'Well,' said Mrs Meadows, this added problem making her hesitate, 'we go home tomorrow, you know.'

'I'm sure something could be arranged. We could call for Lavinia tomorrow morning. There would be no need for a maid as she could share Sophy's. Then when you wished Lavinia to return home perhaps we could meet somewhere to save you driving all the way from Kent.'

'Well, thank you,' said Mrs Meadows, feeling she couldn't refuse the offer. When the proposed treat was suggested to the girls Lavinia thought it would be lovely to relax away from the family whom she thought she had let down so badly. Sophy was thrilled too and so it all was arranged.

Meanwhile Sir Nicholas had returned to Sinclair House in Surrey after six years absence. He wondered how it would affect him and Mr Bradley felt a tautness in him as they neared their destination. But Sir Nicholas alighted from the coach with only a glance at the beautiful brick built house, which glowed in the early evening sun before him. He helped Mr Bradley down from the carriage and as they turned they found the front doors had been opened and various members of the staff had appeared to welcome Sir

Nicholas. They were all smiling and looked so pleased to see him that he tried to relax and greet them as he should. As he went indoors he was still accompanied by Mr Bradley, who tried to make things easier by saying: 'This is Mr Donald, I expect you remember him,' and 'this is Mrs Lacey, the housekeeper, you know,' and so it went on.

Sir Nicholas was surprised that everyone seemed so pleased to see him, which made things easier for him. He was shown not to his old room but to the master bedroom. He wondered how he felt taking over his father's domain, but apart from small things, the place looked different through the eyes of a twenty-four-year-old to that of an unhappy eighteen.

It was before the evening meal that he decided to go outside. This was something he had to do alone, to put the ghosts to rest before bedtime. Mr Bradley saw him go and sat down to await his return. Sir Nicholas strode down the wide pathway, now gravelled, away from the house. As he came to the bend, he stopped. Someone had planted a large rose tree which framed a stone plaque on which were the simple words, 'In memory of Sir Julian and Lady Mary Sinclair.'

Sir Nicholas's mind went back to when he was sixteen years old. His Mama had said they were a threesome and always would be. For some reason he didn't know about, she couldn't bear any more children but the three of them had been happy together. His father had an heir in Nicholas and loved his wife very much. It had been a wonderful time until that day when Sir Julian and Lady Mary decided to visit friends nearby, taking out the open carriage with a recently purchased young horse. Lady Mary, an experienced horsewoman, decided to drive and with her husband and groom only, started out. Evidently, the horse was skittish that morning and dashed off before Lady Mary was ready. The carriage wheel hit a stone and Sir Julian and Lady Mary were thrown out while the groom was dragged along as the horse dashed wildly forward. Sadly, all died of head injuries. Afterwards it was wondered why the groom hadn't held the horse's head until all were ready.

Sir Nicholas, of course, was heartbroken. He wouldn't eat and just shut himself in his room. Eventually, Mr and Mrs Beaumont visited, who were distant relations of the Sinclairs. They said they would stay with Nicholas and look after him until he was better. But they didn't do much to help him with his grief and looked to their own interests instead. When he turned eighteen and became legally entitled to manage his inheritance, he brought in his lawyers and proved the Beaumonts were spending his money to feather their own nest. He told them to leave and eventually a rather bitter and cynical Sir Nicholas left Sinclair House for his family's residence in London.

Although he still felt sad for the loss of his wonderful parents, he now felt he could perhaps find interest in the lovely old seventeenth-century house once more and hopefully bring it back to be the happy dwelling it once was. He returned to find Mr Bradley waiting for him, who could tell that the worst part of returning for Sir Nicholas had been dealt with.

During the next few days Sir Nicholas attended to the

business of repairing his house inside and out with the people concerned. He took particular interest in the inside decoration of all the rooms, even the servants' quarters, and anything else that needed doing. This all took longer than he anticipated but he didn't mind for he found he was enjoying himself. The inside work progressing satisfactorily, he next turned his attention to the gardens. They were formal in the main with topiary hedges, but there was one small area that just grew wild flowers including primroses, bluebells, cowslips, daisies, buttercups and others depending on the time of year. This was his mother's special place, as she loved the free growing informality of it. Sir Nicholas found the gardener, an elderly man, to thank him and to ask him to continue to grow any wild flowers there in future. The gardener was pleased to continue, probably remembering Lady Sinclair. Last of all Sir Nicholas viewed the river, which flowed at the end of his property. Here he remembered playing in a boat as a boy, much to the alarm of his mother.

The days hurried by and Sir Nicholas, eventually satisfied that everything was progressing as it should, decided to return to London. He had been away much longer than he had intended.

CHAPTER SEVENTEEN

THE FOLLOWING MORNING found the Meadows family gathered together in the drawing room awaiting the arrival of the Gilberts. The servants had been sent back to Kent by a hired carriage with the main luggage, leaving the family with little to worry about apart from Lavinia, who had chosen her most suitable dresses for her stay with Sophy and other personal things which she had packed in the portmanteau that was now sitting at her feet. She wished they would hurry up and come. Her Mama was beginning to be jittery now the Gilberts were a little later than expected, and she gave Lavinia pieces of advice about what to wear and when and what to do when she went here or there. Lavinia, having heard it all before, gripped her fingers together to stop herself from replying sharply. Her Papa, noticing his daughter's problem, at certain moments, when his wife wasn't looking, winked at her. Dear Papa.

At last there was the sound of the clip clop of horses' hooves coming to a stop outside and John rushed to the window. 'Oh, thank goodness, they are here,' he said.

'John!' said his father sharply as he went to open the door himself.

Only Mrs Gilbert and Sophy alighted from the carriage.

'I'm sorry we are late,' smiled Mrs Gilbert, 'but we were held up by a carriage stretched across the road. If only people would learn to drive properly! However we are here now. Are you ready, Lavinia dear?'

Without more talking Lavinia kissed her parents, said farewell to the boys and entered the Gilberts' coach with a sigh of relief. It was a pleasant morning and Lavinia enjoyed looking at the scenery as they travelled at a smart pace. As it was all new to her Sophy pointed out places of interest like the park, various shops and where they would go and Lavinia noticed that like any other part of London she had seen, there were the rough areas too. In next to no time, though, with Sophy chattering all the way, they had arrived at their destination which Lavinia was pleased to see was quiet.

The house seemed large to Lavinia with a long driveway to the rear and as they came to a standstill a servant appeared to pick up Lavinia's luggage. Mrs Gilbert said, as they entered the house, 'Now Sophy, I shall leave you to show Lavinia to her room and see that she is comfortable. Also you are to introduce her to Moffatt and show her where certain rooms are. Anything you require, Lavinia, just ask.'

'How kind your Mama is,' said Lavinia as they mounted the stairs.

'This is your room and that one is mine,' said Sophy as she pointed to a door on the other side of the corridor. 'If you want anything let me know by just knocking on the door. I hope you like your room. It used to be my elder sister's.'

Lavinia found it to be charming, decorated in delicate pinks and creams with curtains round the bed to match. The view from the window was of the pretty garden at the back. 'Oh, Sophy, it is lovely. Thank you.' She began to take off her bonnet and pelisse when there was a knock on the door.

Sophy opened it. 'Oh, Moffatt, it's you. Do come in and let me introduce you to Lavinia, Miss Meadows.'

Moffatt was older than the girls but neat and tidy with a friendly disposition. She gave a little curtsey to Lavinia who smiled at her. 'How do you do? Please tell me what I am to call you.'

'Just Moffatt, Miss.'

'She is the dearest creature and such a help in many ways,' said Sophy with a mischievous smile.

'Don't be giving away secrets, now, Miss Sophy,' admonished Moffatt.

'She turns a blind eye when I'm out with Martin,' whispered Sophy. 'She's a dear.'

'You be careful what you're saying, now,' said Moffatt.

'Oh Lavinia won't tell, will you Lavinia?'

'I don't know anything to tell, do I?' laughed her friend.

'Now do come along. Moffatt will unpack for you and I want to show you the garden,' said Sophy.

Lavinia settled in to her new lifestyle with no problem. Mr and Mrs Gilbert were kind and treated Lavinia like their daughter. They were told of the invitations there were, like musical evenings, informal and friendly dances, and outings during the daytime. There was no pressure to look for a husband, just enjoyment in a pleasant, relaxed way. This was what Lavinia needed. Trying to please everyone was a hard task and to be expected only to enjoy herself in a happy atmosphere was wonderful.

Sir Nicholas, on the other hand, was back once more in London looking through all the invitations to the last balls of the season and theatre engagements with friends. In one way he was pleased to be back but he had enjoyed overseeing the renovations to Sinclair House. He was sure he had been right to refrain from visiting it for a few years and although he still mourned the loss of his parents, he felt the hurt was over and he could enjoy going there again. Now, it would be agreeable if he found someone suitable to marry to share it with him. But whom? The sweet face of Miss Buttercup came to mind. He turned the idea over and over in his mind and found it pleasing and after further thought realised that perhaps he had loved her for some time although he hadn't really appreciated his emotions or thought about hers. Now how should he go about this? See her first or visit her Papa? Yes, he thought, he should pay a visit to Mr Meadows, which was the proper way, of course and no doubt Lavinia would prefer it Not that the propriety of the situation worried Sir Nicholas, but he was conscious of a flash of pleasure in his own consideration of Lavinia's feelings. He decided he would visit the following morning.

Just before eleven o'clock, dressed in a coat of light blue with silver embroidery and with his dark hair tied neatly, he looked at his elegant figure in the mirror. He decided he could do no more and indeed any young lady, or any older ones for that matter, would swoon if they were proposed to by him, however dressed.

As the carriage drew up outside the house in Mount Street he waited for the servant to climb down and to knock on the door. After some minutes it was opened by what looked like a cleaning lady who informed him no one lived there. She was cleaning it, she said, after the last people who had hired it had left. This news didn't please Sir Nicholas. As he was driven back home he thought someone should have let him know, but after further consideration he realised he couldn't have expected it as he had disappeared into Surrey without telling anyone. He didn't have time, as it was a quick decision to accompany Mr Bradley. He felt a premonition as though everything was not as it should be. Had Miss Meadows ever told him where she lived? He didn't think so—she hadn't had any cause to. So where was he going to find out where she was? Perhaps Lady Waverly might know. She knew most things. He would visit her, now.

By this time it was late morning and Sir Nicholas hoped Lady Waverly was available as the time for morning visits was now over. He was told to wait in one of the downstairs rooms by a servant who said he would see if Lady Waverly would receive him. Sir Nicholas was left to kick his heels and look at the numerous portraits on the wall, which he had seen many times before. However, a few minutes later the servant returned saying that Lady Waverly would be delighted to see him in the withdrawing room.

Telling the servant he needn't bother to accompany him as he knew the way, Sir Nicholas climbed the stairs two at a time, knocked on the door and walked in. He bowed. 'Thank you for seeing me, dear lady,' he said as he kissed her hand.

'Good morning, Nicholas. It is nice to see you and dressed so beautifully too. Sit down and tell me why you are here.'

'I have been in Surrey putting Sinclair House in order. Mr Bradley came himself as he needed my permission for work to be done and I hadn't—er—been there since...'

'The accident,' Lady Waverly supplied. 'Well, better late than never, as they say.'

'Yes, well, I decided that if I was to marry it should be a welcoming house and not one falling to pieces.'

'Quite right,' said Lady Waverly obligingly. 'And are you to be married?'

'I went to Mount Street where the Meadows family were living and...'

'And,' prompted Lady Waverly.

'The family have left and gone home, evidently. I don't know where that is and I wondered if you did, that is all.'

'I see. I'm sorry, I don't know their address. I can ask around, of course, but it will take a while.'

'I thought as you invited them that evening you might know.'

'And you think Miss Meadows would like to marry you, Nicholas? You would have to be very kind to her, you know.'

'I know. Do you think I would treat my wife any other

way, Ma'am?'

'I think you could be just as you should if you wanted to, dear. Is this just a quick decision or has it been in your mind for some time?'

'No. But when I decided this is the time I should be married and my houses should have a beautiful mistress, the face which came into my mind was the sweet face of Lavinia Meadows.'

'I see. It's a big step to take, dear. Are you sure?'

'Yes. The more I think of it the more I like the idea. I find I like being with her. She is a mixture of thoughtfulness, kindness and mischief and she has courage.'

'Well, that is an accolade indeed so there is no more to be said, is there?' Lady Waverly smiled at him. 'I think it is time you settled down, you know, and Miss Meadows is a sweet girl. Now, I could ask Wills, my husband's secretary, if he has the Meadows' address. He organised it all, you know.' She rang the bell and a servant came in answer. 'Could you ask Mr Wills to see me please? Now.'

It wasn't long before Wills arrived. 'Do you remember inviting the Meadows family to my ball, Wills?'

'The name sounds familiar, Madam.'

'Could you check their address please and let me know. It is most important.'

Wills bowed and left, promising to let her ladyship know as soon as he could. But when he returned all he could tell her was their London address of Mount Street.

'Are you in a hurry, Nicholas? But of course you are,' she said, answering her own question. 'Let me think a moment. Ah! Have you been invited to Lady Buxton's ball tonight? I think it's the last of the season. If so there will be two ladies there who will know everything about everyone. It would be worth a try, anyway.'

'Yes, it would, wouldn't it? Thank you.' Soon after Sir Nicholas left.

Lavinia was enjoying herself. Although she was sure Mrs Gilbert kept an eye on them, much of the girls' supervision was by Moffatt, Lavinia thought. Mrs Gilbert let them enjoy themselves by shopping, walking in the park and meeting friends. Occasionally, she accompanied them but it was usually Moffatt. Sophy treated her like an elder sister and very soon so did Lavinia. Moffatt never overstepped the mark but was friendly, made sensible suggestions as to what to visit and gave her opinion on whether certain things, like pieces of jewellery, were suitable for young ladies to wear. The weather was pleasantly warm and so the days, busy but enjoyable, passed by. There was no time to think during the day, which Lavinia was pleased about, but on retiring at night, after Mrs Gilbert kindly came in to say 'Goodnight' and to ask if there was anything she needed, the picture of a certain gentleman came to mind. Lavinia went over in her mind how wonderfully he danced, how kind he could be if he wished and finally went to sleep with the thought of his kissing her on her first meeting with him.

Sir Nicholas would have been delighted to have known

of Lavinia's bedtime thoughts but only one thing filled his mind at the moment and that was to find Lavinia and her father. He tried to put all this to the back of his mind, however, as he entered Lady Buxton's ballroom. She was delighted to see him and he complimented her on the many couples who were dancing, as this was the last ball of the season and many had already left for the coast or countryside.

The ballroom looked delightful as it was decorated with fresh flowers and very light gossamer-like drapes. The chandeliers shone, which told of the hard work of Lady Buxton's staff. Sir Nicholas was soon joined by some of his friends and talk turned to what they all intended to do this summer and whom they would visit, from delightful young relatives to ancient crones. Sir Nicholas joined in the general jollity but all the time his eyes were searching for those two grand ladies.

It was while he was dancing the cotillion that he saw Effie and Dru tucked away behind some greenery where they sat on comfortable cushioned chairs. They were looking as they usually did, with hair piled high, low necklines on their dresses and those ridiculous tiny shoes. When the dance was finished and at a convenient moment Sir Nicholas strolled over to greet them and in return he was entertained to much coquetry and the use of their large fans.

Sir Nicholas asked them if they were well, complimented them on their appearances and hoped he could obtain some champagne for them. They thanked him and rewarded him by turning the conversation to Lavinia. 'It is a shame Miss Meadows had to return home, isn't it, Effie?' asked Dru.

'You danced so well together, Sir Nicholas.'

He bowed. 'Thank you. I didn't know she had returned home,' he said.

'Yes,' said Dru, 'we asked her where she lived and it isn't too far away.'

'Oh, no,' said Effie. 'It is only a small place called Limwood on the Kent border, you know.'

'I see,' said Sir Nicholas. 'I thank you, ladies. Enjoy your champagne.' He bowed then winked at them, which made them retire coyly behind their fans, giggling like two young girls.

Soon after Sir Nicholas left the ball, complimenting the hostess and pleased to have found out just what he wanted to know.

CHAPTER EIGHTEEN

THE NEXT DAY, after a leisurely breakfast, Sir Nicholas gave orders for his coach to be brought round before lunch. He said he was going into Kent and luncheon could be eaten somewhere along the way. He told his valet to pack what was needed for two nights and to be ready to accompany him. Roberts wished to see him about some business affairs but Sir Nicholas said that unless they were urgent they could wait for a day or two, or if not, he was to deal with them as he saw fit. Roberts, used to this answer, bowed and said nothing. He could tell Sir Nicholas's thoughts were elsewhere and hoped he found the address he wanted in Kent, which seemed so important to him.

The coach was brought round at the appropriate time, the horses fresh and ready to go and Sir Nicholas was about to climb aboard when he looked round at Roberts with a smile. 'Wish me well,' he said.

'Indeed I do, sir,' Roberts replied instantly. No doubt Sir Nicholas thought he had second sight but he assumed he was to visit Miss Meadows's father.

The door closed and the coachman, holding the horses on a tight rein with great skill, drove around the square and into the busy London streets. When they were clear of these he let the horses have their heads and they travelled more comfortably along the roads to the east, which hopefully led to Limwood on the outskirts of Kent.

The Meadows family was back home and in their usual routines. Mary Meadows felt happier now away from London and in her own home, and where she knew everyone in the village. She didn't begrudge the time spent in London for either of her two daughters and she was now over her disappointment about Lavinia not finding a husband. She didn't like admitting to her friends of her daughter's failure and she knew they would gossip but it couldn't be helped and everything would settle down to normality eventually and in a short while all would be forgotten. But Mary couldn't resist telling her friends how they had all been invited to Lady Waverly's ball and how Lavinia had danced with Sir Nicholas while everyone else watched them. And that now she was staying with friends in Hammersmith.

Percy Meadows was also pleased to be back home where he could stroll in his garden, chat to his friends and take part in village life once more.

The boys met their friends again and told them of their adventures in London. John was particularly pleased to show them his treasures, as he called them. He told them how he had had to dig for them in the muddy edges of the River Thames and they were greatly impressed. He boasted of being covered in mud and not finding his way home until the following day, but he didn't say how frightened he had been.

Edward described his fight and proved the outcome by showing his scar. He told them how Sir Nicholas had killed the two antagonists and saved Edward's life and how he had taken him to his own home and paid for a surgeon to attend him.

In Hammersmith the next morning, although the sun shone it wasn't quite such a warm day. One or two tiny dark clouds travelled overhead but Sophy and Lavinia hoped it would soon brighten up. Sophy wondered where they could go and after much thought Moffatt suggested a short walk across the local park to a street not too far away where there were some special shops.

'I'm sure you would like it, Lavinia, and the people are all beautifully dressed,' said Sophy. 'It used to be called Yew Tree Walk but isn't anymore for some reason. The shops are for looking at only as what they sell is all very expensive but there is a heavenly jewellers and we could look for our engagement rings, couldn't we?' she laughed.

'You can, of course,' said Lavinia. 'And I will see if what you choose is suitable for you,' she finished primly.

'Thank you, Mama,' said Sophy curtseying with a giggle.

'There are some small dress shops and little boutiques, too,' said Moffatt.

'Also,' said Sophy, 'there are some sweetmeat shops and places to drink coffee, you know.'

'It all sounds delightful so we must dress in our best. What will you wear, Sophy? Will this pink dress of mine be suitable for me, do you think?' asked Lavinia.

'Oh, yes,' said her friend, 'that one is very pretty, and I shall wear blue. My bonnet which matches has pink and white flowers on it so it will be suitable I think, and we will look well together.'

'If there were some showers we can always shelter in a doorway, or there is a small arcade showing paintings which we could visit,' said Moffatt.

After breakfast, and telling Mr and Mrs Gilbert where they were going with Moffatt, they set off.

The three of them chatted all the way to the shops. What one didn't know the others did and so with much giggling they enjoyed the walk through the park. After this, of course, they quietened down and behaved as their mamas would have expected them to and Moffatt became their mentor once more.

The street looked delightful and although there were boys sweeping a crossing, there really wasn't very much dirt to sweep away apart from that left by the occasional horse. The street was too narrow for carriages so it was reasonably safe to walk along looking in the shop windows. These were charming, their architecture, in some cases, dating back to a previous age but all were clean and displaying modern and old books, beautiful clothes, sweetmeats and, of course, jewellery.

Lavinia found herself wishing for more money in her purse to buy gifts for the family as they pointed out the most desirable things to each other, but all were beyond their allowances. As time went on they found more people walking and visiting the shops and friends meeting with much bowing and curtseying. Then there was a little scream as four young ladies with their attendants noticed Sophy.

'Oh, Sophy,' called one, 'how lovely to see you again.' They crowded round their friend chattering like magpies. Sophy introduced Lavinia and then began to bring them up to date with her news. They reciprocated and, knowing Sophy was to be engaged soon, one of the girls showed off her own engagement ring. Lavinia smiled and spoke when she could but this was difficult, as they all seemed to be talking at once. Moffatt and the girls' duennas drew slightly away from them and talked quietly to each other while keeping an eye on their charges.

After a while, Lavinia, not knowing the people the other girls were talking about, let her mind wander, although she kept a smile on her face. But more and more she found her attention on other people passing by. They were, for the most, beautifully dressed as Sophy had said, but then as she looked she saw something that wiped the smile off her face. Two elegantly dressed young men stopped on the opposite side of the street. They began to talk to the gentleman there and when they laughingly said goodbye with much bowing, one of them quietly and deftly removed a purse from the gentleman's pocket. They bowed again and moved on. Lavinia couldn't believe her eyes. Then she saw them bump into another gentleman whom they didn't know, evidently, as there was much bowing and apologising and again Lavinia saw a purse and a gold watch disappear from the gentleman into one of their pockets. It was all done so neatly and Lavinia wondered if she was really seeing pickpockets at work. Was her eyesight better than others? Lavinia was horrified and looked round to see if anyone else had noticed what was going on, but everyone was just busy with their own shopping and talking to the people they accompanied.

Lavinia followed the men with her eyes, wondering how many more people they would rob and should she do something about it, when, as if they could feel her gaze upon them, they looked straight at her. Lavinia's eyes opened even wider as she saw that one of the men was M de Craon. She was shocked. She didn't know where to look. Sophy and her friends were still laughing and chatting so all Lavinia could think of doing was to turn round to look in the shop window of the jewellers behind her. She concentrated hard on looking at the rings there but the sight of those men thieving had shaken her.

Suddenly there was a light touch on her arm and she looked up into the eyes of M de Craon. He smiled and said pleasantly enough: 'Miss Meadows, you are looking at the rings. Let me show you those in this window just round the corner.' He indicated a smaller window in the alley by the side of the shop. He spoke English without any French accent so what did this mean?

'Oh, thank you but as you see I am with friends.' She tried to edge her way back to Sophy and Moffatt but the other gentleman with M de Craon stood the other side of her, blocking any movement she might make.

'I think you will find the jewellery in this window more interesting,' said M de Craon, taking her arm. She didn't wish to go with him. The side of the shop did indeed have a small window showing jewellery and she didn't want to make a vulgar scene, so she moved just a little way with him, wondering if he was going to try and explain his actions to her. She glimpsed a narrow passage that led to the backs of the buildings along the street. She had no time to cry out as a hand was placed firmly over her mouth and she was lifted up and carried down that passage. She tried to struggle but she was just held tighter. She felt she couldn't breathe and she couldn't move either.

'That one will do,' she heard M de Craon say and there was a sound of a heavy door being opened. She was released abruptly and pushed inside so that she fell onto the floor. 'Enjoy your day. We will see you later, Miss Meadows,' he said. As she picked herself up, she heard the door shut and a bolt slide into place. She was left in the dark. When she had recovered a little from the shock and her breathing was nearly normal again she looked round and could see nothing but the darkness in front of her. Evidently there were no windows. She managed to get up and tried to find her way back to the door. She was able to rattle it a little but could not find a handle or bolt on her side. There was a smell and Lavinia thought it was of coal. The darkness had lifted slightly as her eyes accustomed themselves to the dimness. She could see no coal, only dirt. How long would she be kept here? She tried shouting but she felt there was no one to hear, as her voice was muffled by the thick walls. No doubt this was someone's coalhouse, but as she moved carefully around there didn't seem to be any coal, just the smell of it. Perhaps if there had been some coal someone would come for it and find her. If not? She didn't know what to do and hoped there were no rats. She sat down and hugged her knees, as it was decidedly chilly. From time to time she tried shouting again but her voice sounded thin in the enclosed space. M de Craon said he would see her later. But how late would that be? She began to shiver from fear and the creeping cold. Would anyone let her out or would she just get weaker and weaker and then die? She must be strong, she told herself. Sophy and Moffatt would look for her, they might even find her. But would they think of looking at the back of the shops? They would alert Sophy's parents and they would know what to do and who to tell. All she had to do was to keep as warm as she could. Perhaps it would help if she thought of her family. Then she thought of Sir Nicholas. Where was he? He had left London, she knew. She thought he liked her so why did he go away without saying anything to her? She might never see him again and he certainly wouldn't know she was here. Then her tears began to fall and she sobbed until she was utterly exhausted.

CHAPTER NINETEEN

THE HOSTELRY Sir Nicholas stayed at that night was better than he had anticipated. It had supplied him with a comfortable bedchamber, excellent food and decent wines, which he thought could only be had in London's best hotels. He was pleased to have found out this was not the case and next morning he awoke in a good humour, much to his servants' surprise and delight. He had a leisurely breakfast and then, following instructions from the landlord, Sir Nicholas set out for Limwood and the house of the Meadows family. It was a pleasant morning with the sun shining and the countryside looked green and fresh. It made one feel good to fill the lungs with clean air.

Sir Nicholas travelled at a leisurely pace, as there were not many miles before they came to Limwood and he didn't wish to arrive before eleven o'clock thinking that was a reasonable time and the usual time for morning calls.

They were soon driving down the wide street. Lime trees flanked each side, which obviously gave the village its name. The coachman brought the horse to a halt while his groom enquired from a group of locals where Mr Meadows' house could be found. He was told it wasn't too far away, just round the corner where he would eventually see a gateway on the right, which led to the house. It was hidden from the road by trees. The coachman followed these instructions and he was soon drawing up before a pleasant looking house in its own grounds. It wasn't large, Sir Nicholas noticed, but it was well looked after.

As Sir Nicholas jumped down, a door opened and a servant came towards him.

'Good morning, sir.'

'Good morning. Is Mr Meadows at home and if so may I see him?'

'Yes, of course, sir. Please come this way.' He led Sir Nicholas to a door while another servant came to lead the carriage away.

Sir Nicholas was shown into a sunny morning room. 'Please sir, who shall I say has called?'

Sir Nicholas told him. 'Please be seated, sir. Mr Meadows isn't far away.' He bowed and left the room.

Two minutes later the door opened again and Percy Meadows entered. He bowed. 'Good morning, Sir Nicholas. What a surprise to see you. Can I offer you a glass of port or sherry?'

'Thank you, port if you please. What an attractive part of the country you live in and the village, what I saw of it, looked charming. I hope I haven't arrived at an inconvenient time?'

'Not at all. I'm pleased to see you. We don't stand on ceremony in this part of the world, you know.' He handed Sir Nicholas his glass of port and placed a small table by his side, then sat opposite his guest. They talked about the countryside and London. Sir Nicholas asked after the health of Mrs Meadows and Edward and John. When Percy had answered these questions Sir Nicholas continued.

'Perhaps you can guess why I have come to see you, Mr Meadows? It is to ask you for your daughter's hand in marriage.'

Percy smiled broadly. 'I hoped it would be that and I would be delighted—if Lavinia agrees, of course.'

Sir Nicholas smiled. 'Thank you. I am quite happy if you wish to ask me any questions but I must tell you I am able to support a wife and a possible family quite comfortably.'

'I'm sure of it,' smiled Percy.

'I have been these last few weeks in Surrey. I have a house there to which I shall be pleased to invite you and any of your family.'

'Thank you and I am sure that they all will be pleased to see you before you leave us today.'

'I believe Mrs Meadows doesn't view me with such confidence as you do, Mr Meadows?'

'Mothers, I suppose, have special thoughts for their daughters. Would you like to see her? But I must tell you Lavinia is not here at the moment. She is staying with friends in Hammersmith until the end of this week, I think. But I can give you their address if you would like me to?'

Sir Nicholas naturally looked disappointed. 'That is, of course, inconvenient,' he said. 'But perhaps I could visit you again when your daughter has returned?'

'Certainly you may and when we know her answer we

must consider the dowry. Now let me see if my wife can join us.' He rang the bell, which was answered by George who went to find Mary Meadows. She was in the kitchen at that moment talking to Cook when George found her and said Mr Meadows had asked for her to join him in the morning room as he had a visitor. She hurriedly made her way immediately, checking in the hall mirror that she looked neat and tidy.

As she entered Sir Nicholas stood up and bowed. She acknowledged this with a small curtsey. 'Why, Sir Nicholas, this is a surprise! Please sit down. I see my husband has offered you a drink. Can I offer you any other refreshment?'

'Thank you, no,' smiled Sir Nicholas.

'Sir Nicholas came to see us to ask if he may pay his addresses to Lavinia, my dear,' her husband said, not mincing matters. 'I've given my approval but he seems to need yours as well.'

'Oh, oh I see,' said Mary, all this coming as a bit of a shock.

'Mrs Meadows,' said Sir Nicholas, 'I know you are concerned for your daughter and quite rightly so. But I hope you will agree with your husband. I am told she is not here to answer for herself but if she looks favourably on my suit, I hope you both will be pleased with her decision. If there are any questions you would like to ask me, please do so.'

'I think Sir Nicholas is in earnest, my dear,' said Percy. 'Lavinia is a sensible girl and I think if she says "yes" to Sir Nicholas' proposal we should abide by her decision.'

'Well in that case, what can I say but that I agree with

my husband,' said Mary.

'My father, you know, respected my mother and treated her with kindness and I would certainly do the same for your daughter,' said Sir Nicholas gently. 'I had hoped to have spoken to you both after Lady Gilmore's ball but I was needed at my house in Surrey urgently so I had to depart early the next morning. It is a comfortable house to visit and my parents loved it. Your boys would like the river, which runs by and there are gardens to enjoy. How are Edward and—and John, I believe?'

'Edward has recovered from his fright very well thanks to you, sir, and John is the same as ever, forever in a scrape,' said their father. 'Now it is nearly lunchtime—would you like to stay and join us, Sir Nicholas? Please do, the boys would love to meet you again, I know. I'm sure your coachman and groom would be pleased of something to eat too and no doubt the kitchen staff will attend to that,' said Percy.

'Thank you, that is very kind of you both,' said Sir Nicholas with his attractive smile. 'And I would like to meet the boys again very much.'

'I will go and see Cook and tell her to prepare for an extra guest. Excuse me, gentlemen.' And Mary hurried from the room.

'I think we managed that particular hurdle very well, don't you?' said Percy

'She won't regret her decision,' said Sir Nicholas.

'Before you go we must discuss the question of my daughter's dowry and I will give you the Gilberts' address in case you wish to visit,' said Percy.

There was a knock on the door. It opened slightly and

Edward looked round. 'May John and I come in, Father?'

'Yes, of course. Sir Nicholas is staying for luncheon.'

The boys came in, made their bows and then sat near Sir Nicholas telling him about what they had been doing. He asked the right questions and they were getting on very well when lunch was announced. He had enjoyed their company, he was surprised to find, and realised what he had missed in his own life.

Sometime later Sir Nicholas took his leave. He had enjoyed his time with the Meadows family, especially with the boys, who made him feel he was part of the family. How he wished he had experienced this when he was young. It was disappointing Lavinia wasn't present, of course. He decided to return home and visit Lavinia the next day.

Meanwhile, Mr Gilbert had been back to the shops where Lavinia had disappeared and asked questions of the shop owners and searched every nook and cranny as far as he could. When he finished he was puzzled indeed but decided to go to Bow Street to see if someone there could help who was used to looking for missing persons. Then on the following day he would have the unenviable task of travelling to Kent to let the Meadows family know the shocking news about their daughter.

Lavinia would have been pleased to have known someone was doing something but she was feeling very cold, light headed and weak. She had tried walking around and waving her arms about to keep warm but she couldn't see well enough and caught her hands on the rough walls. Then her stomach groaned telling her she was hungry and she had a feeling the saliva in her mouth had dried up. She sat on the floor, hugging her knees, which she drew up before her. She kept thinking that no one knew where she was, apart from those two men. What if they didn't return and she just starved to death? She didn't want to die. Realising the horror of it all she burst into tears and wept and wept until she was exhausted. Then mercifully, her head drooped and she slept.

How long she stayed like that she didn't know but she was awakened by a clatter outside and eventually the door was wrenched open. Lavinia raised her head and found she was dizzy but she could make out two men, one of whom was holding a lantern.

'Up you come,' one said, whom she vaguely recognised as being M de Craon.

She didn't say anything as her throat was dry and she felt disorientated. He didn't say anymore but threw a dark cover over her, which didn't smell too clean and nearly choked her. She was completely covered and she tried to remove it as she could hardly breathe. Two arms came round her and held her tightly and then she was lifted off her feet and slung over his shoulder. Anyone out at that late hour would think he was just carrying a bundle of clothes. His accomplice shut and bolted the door and picked up the lantern. Without speaking they walked the length of the street. It was dark and all the shops were closed and only the light from the lantern the man carried showed them the way. At the end of the street, a ragamuffin held an old horse harnessed to a cart. The man with the lantern tossed him a coin and the boy scampered off leaving M de Craon to climb up onto the seat with Lavinia while his friend let go of the horse and jumped quickly up onto the cart. They drove off.

All this time Lavinia hadn't the strength to move and she was more concerned with trying to breathe through what she vaguely thought must be a smelly horse blanket. It wasn't too long before they stopped once more and Lavinia heard one of the men muttering. The blanket was taken off her and she was lifted up, none too carefully, by M de Craon. She took a deep breath of air and felt better but when she saw what was before her she gasped in fright as they were standing on the edge of the River Thames with water lapping round their feet. Far away were a few lights but immediately before her was only blackness. She could hear an occasional craft moving in the distance and showing a feeble light, otherwise all was quiet and dark. Lavinia wondered if she could move for she was very tired and stiff but M de Craon lifted her up roughly and turned with her so she could just make out his friend holding on to a small rowing boat that had been left on the bank and which he had pushed into the water. Lavinia was dumped at the bottom of the boat with a hand firmly planted on her back to keep her there.

'Where are we going?' she managed to ask.

There was no reply and only the movement of the boat on the water gave her the answer. She began to scream and got her face slapped for her pains but she didn't care, she just screamed and screamed again and again. Then worse came. She was grabbed by strong hands and thrown over the side into the cold, dark water. She managed to scream once more before she went under.

The men in the boat headed back to the shore as quickly as possible.

CHAPTER TWENTY

'**JOSH**, did you hear something?'

'Yes, Pa, I think so.'

'I expect we had better take a look,' Ben sighed.

The ferryman and his son had finished for the day after taking an older couple home across the River Thames. Now they were looking forward to a rest and a well earned meal. It was difficult to see anything in the dark but they had a lantern, which helped a little, but it wasn't very bright. They could manage to see if anyone was floating in the water, however. Of course, it might be someone dumping things they didn't want. The river was a good place for getting rid of rubbish but unfortunately people were sometimes included too.

Josh rowed as hard as he could to where they thought they had heard the cry while his father held the lantern. They were used to scanning the dark water but they weren't always successful in finding what they wanted. However, Josh shouted out. 'There, something is moving!' And he rowed rapidly to the spot.

'Hold on to the oars, Pa, while I find out what it is.' He bent over the side of the boat, grabbed at the thing he had seen in the water and heaved. It was a good thing that Josh, like his father, was strong, with muscles well developed from rowing. He struggled as the bundle was heavy and sodden with water but he managed to lift it aboard.

'Why, it's a girl,' said his father. 'Lay her face down, Josh. Now take the oars and row like mad to the shore. I'll see what I can do to put some life into her.' He knelt down carefully in the boat and pressed her back where her lungs were to try to get her breathing again. Meanwhile, Josh pulled hard on the oars. At the shore he left his Pa to secure the boat and he picked up the wet figure. His father followed as quickly as possible.

'Take her to your Ma's, Josh, and get your Molly to come over to our house to help.'

'Come quickly, Ma!' shouted Josh as he went in the door and placed Lavinia carefully on the floor.

Sal, his mother, a deep bosomed woman with dark hair beneath her white mobcap, came hurrying from the kitchen. 'Good gracious, is she dead?'

'We don't know,' said her husband, 'but let us see if we can revive her, Sal, shall we?'

'Poor little soul, what did she go and get herself drowned for?'

Ben continued trying to get the girl to cough up the water she had taken in. He worked hard and was getting warm with his efforts but he continued and at last a little sigh came from the drenched figure on the floor.

'I've done it, I think I've done it, Sal!'

'Well done, Ben, well done. Turn her over and let her

have a good cough and then when we've given her a drop of brandy I'll get her warm and dry.'

Josh's wife, Molly, came in. 'Gracious, we had better get her out of those wet clothes otherwise everywhere will be steamed up,' she said.

Ben found the bottle of brandy and Molly tried to get a few drops into the girl's mouth.

Then Sal sent the men out of the kitchen, found two blankets in the cupboard and she and Molly proceeded to cut off Lavinia's wet clothes, which were sticking to her. She thought it a shame to cut them off but the sooner they were off her body the better. They dried her as well as they could with towels. The rubbing seemed to warm her up and she began to move a little. They tucked the blankets round her and rolled up a towel to support her head and wet hair.

'You try giving her a drop more brandy, Molly,' said Sal, 'while I wipe up the floor. I've put her clothes in the sink. I'll dry them but they won't be much good, I shouldn't think.'

'She's coming round,' said Molly. 'Hello, luv, it's all right, you're safe and sound.'

But Lavinia, opening her eyes and seeing a strange face above her and being covered in blankets as she lay on the floor, started to struggle, her eyes darting from side to side.

Sal came back and knelt beside her and took hold of her hands, which were clawing at the blankets. 'Everything will be all right, dear. My husband found you in the river and brought you back here. When you feel better we'll take you home to where you live. And no one here is going to hurt you. You are with friends. Now would you like a little soup? It will make you feel better.'

Lavinia didn't answer and she still looked frightened to death but after a few spoonfuls of the soup she relaxed in the warmth of the kitchen and eventually slept.

Molly went back home to give Josh his meal while Ben and Sal sat down to theirs. They were used to late suppers, as the job of ferryman sometimes led to late hours. But it was the only work Ben knew, having worked with his ferryman father before him.

'We shall have to make a more comfortable bed for the poor girl,' said Sal. 'She can't sleep on the floor all night. I wonder who she is—her clothes are quite good quality. It was a shame to cut them.'

'Haven't we a spare mattress somewhere, one that Josh used to have as a boy?' asked Ben.

'Oh, I think it's in that cupboard upstairs.'

'Then I'll bring it down after supper,' said Ben.

'I shall stay with the girl overnight and then we'll see if she will tell us where she's from,' said Sal.

So Lavinia was made more comfortable on the horsehair mattress on the floor and covered in the blankets. With a little food she was warm and so she slept again. She was a little perturbed when she saw Ben but Sal told her he was her husband and wouldn't hurt a fly. He had left the room as soon as possible as he didn't want to 'worrit the poor child,' he had said.

Sal sat until daylight broke but instead of improving the girl became restless. Her temperature rose and she became

196

delirious calling out as she lived her nightmare again. Sal tried to calm her but she thrashed about uncovering herself. She called out for her mama, Sophy and Sir Nicholas. Who these people were poor Sal had no idea.

'The girl should have a doctor. I haven't anything I can give her,' said poor Sal, shaking her head.

'I'll go and see if Josh can help,' said Ben.

Josh and Molly thought it a good idea for one of them to find a doctor. 'I'm sure someone she knows will pay the doctor's bill, if that's what is worrying you,' said Josh to his Pa. 'Do you go to work and I'll find you if I need you.'

So Ben went off as usual leaving Josh to find a doctor and Molly to go and help her mother-in-law with their patient.

Sir Nicholas awoke that morning with a sense of well being, as he would be visiting the Gilberts that very day to ask Lavinia to marry him. He would have to see Mr Gilbert and explain how he had been to Kent to see Lavinia's family and her father had given him permission to pay his addresses to his daughter. Therefore, Sir Nicholas was in a good mood as he breakfasted, read his letters that had arrived and saw Roberts. 'I am going into Hammersmith to see Miss Meadows who is staying with friends there,' he said.

'I hope you find her this time, sir,' smiled Roberts.

'So do I,' said Sir Nicholas.

It was late morning when he set out and very soon his carriage was drawing up outside the Gilberts' house. He trod up the steps, and rapped on the door. When it was opened he asked the servant if he could see Mr Gilbert. He said he would enquire. He left Sir Nicholas in the hall but soon returned and Sir Nicholas was shown into a pleasant parlour where Mrs Gilbert stood waiting for him. She curtseyed. 'Sir Nicholas, I'm sorry to say my husband is not at home at the moment but I wondered if I could help. Will you not be seated?'

'Thank you.' Sir Nicholas sat down, noticing the elegantly furnished room and the lady sitting opposite who looked decidedly worried. He continued. 'I went down to Kent yesterday to see Mr Meadows and he said his daughter was staying with you and that is why I am here. I wondered if I could see her, please?'

Mrs Gilbert looked even more uncomfortable. 'Oh, I see. I'm sorry,' she said, 'you see, she isn't here. My husband is away. He went down to Kent this morning to… to see Mr Meadows. He went to tell them that we do not know where Lavinia is.' She finished in a rush.

Sir Nicholas frowned. 'I don't understand. What do you mean, Madam? Tell me what has happened at once, if you please.'

As concisely as possible Mrs Gilbert told him what had occurred and also that her husband had reported it to Mr Fielding of Bow Street

'Would you like to see my daughter and her servant and hear what they have to say, sir? They are very upset as you can imagine.' She rang a hand bell and as a servant appeared she asked her to find them. Sophy and Moffatt came into the room and when Sophy knew to whom she was curtseying she felt very apprehensive.

'Oh, sir,' she said, 'I am so sorry.'

As Sir Nicholas looked at her, he could tell she hadn't been sleeping well as her eyes were very tired with dark patches beneath and red with crying.

He said as gently as he could: 'Will you please tell me from the beginning what happened? Miss Meadows came to stay with you and...?'

Sophy cleared her throat. 'We decided, Moffatt and I, as the weather wasn't reliable we would take Lavinia to a street which isn't too far away and which has beautiful shops to look at. She was to help me choose an engagement ring, just looking in the window for fun, you know, as I am to be engaged soon. Then some of my friends saw us and...' She couldn't continue.

Moffatt said quietly: 'The four girls were delighted to see Miss Gilbert again and I noticed they chatted together and Miss Meadows was with them, I remember. Their chaperone was known to me and she and I began to talk until she decided it was time they must leave. We waved goodbye and when they had gone we found there was no Miss Meadows. We waited, thinking she had probably seen something in the jewellers' window and had gone inside, perhaps, but when she didn't come we looked in every shop up and down the street. She was nowhere to be seen. We waited, thinking she would return any minute, but she didn't, sir.'

'I see,' said Sir Nicholas with a frown.

Mrs Gilbert took up the story. 'They came home and told us and my husband went himself and checked everywhere. Then he went to Bow Street to report Miss Meadows as a missing person. If there is anything else we can do, that you can think of, sir, we wouldn't hesitate to do it.'

'I must think. Obviously someone has abducted her—but who and why, I cannot understand at the moment,' said Sir Nicholas. He stood up. 'Thank you for seeing me. I must think what to do next. If you find out anything would you please let me know? My card.'

The ladies curtseyed. 'Thank you, Sir Nicholas. We will certainly let you know.'

On his way home Sir Nicholas was thinking hard. How can a young lady disappear like that? Why did she disappear? And who else was involved? What an elusive young lady he had decided to marry!

CHAPTER TWENTY ONE

JOSH was pleased he was a strong man as the area in London where doctors lived entailed a very long walk from the river. He hoped he could find someone who could let him have some medicine even if they declined to travel all the way to his parents' house to see the girl. It would be a shame to let her die now after all the trouble that had been taken by his family to bring her back to life.

At last he found the houses with brass plates outside proclaiming the names of the doctors who resided within. He remembered visiting a doctor a long time ago when his Pa had been ill but he supposed that doctor had left the practice by now and retired. He found a brass plate with two names on it, and he was hopeful that at least one doctor might be at home. He didn't know what the names said as he couldn't read. He went up the steps and rang the bell. The door opened.

'Could I see a doctor, please? It isn't for...' he began but the man just pointed to a row of chairs and went away. No one else was waiting but after a few minutes a young man opened a door and called Josh inside.

'I am Doctor Bush. How can I help?' He sat down behind his desk and indicated a chair where Josh was to sit.

'I haven't come for myself, sir,' he began.

The doctor frowned. 'Oh? Who, then?' He was brisk and to the point.

'Can I explain that my father and I are ferrymen, sir, and last night we picked up a young girl from the river. We were able to get her breathing again but overnight she has developed a fever. My mother has been looking after her as well as possible but she needs medicine to help her. She is delirious and keeps asking for her mother, Sophy, whoever she is and a Sir Nicholas.'

'I see,' said the doctor. 'How will you pay for the medicine? Have you thought of that?'

'Yes, sir. My father and I will have to pay for it and hope whoever she belongs to will repay us. But we must try and save the poor girl.'

'And you say she asks for Sir Nicholas? Would that be Nicholas Sinclair, I wonder?'

'I don't know, sir, but she asks for him more than anyone.' He saw the doctor smiling. 'Do you know him, sir?'

'I've heard of him, like many others, and my father treats Lady Waverly's staff occasionally. I think there is a connection there somewhere. Very well. I will give you some medicine to bring down the fever.' He rang a hand bell and a man in a white coat appeared. The doctor told him what he required and the man nodded and left. Josh was told to wait outside on the chairs again and eventually the bottle of medicine was brought to him. 'Can you read the instructions?' the man asked.

'No. I've no learning, sir, I'm afraid.'

'It says a small spoonful to be given every three hours. Can you remember that?'

'Yes, of course. How much do I owe you?'

Josh handed the money over without a blink but it had cost him and his father two weeks' work to achieve it. He hoped they would be reimbursed but if not, he couldn't let the young lady die—it would be on his conscience forever. He left the surgery and hurried as fast as possible back to his parents' house.

Meanwhile Sir Nicholas was restless. What had happened to his love? After much thought he decided the only thing he could do was to go to Bow Street and see if there was any news. Perhaps someone had seen something or knew more. Once there he did find that some people had had valuables stolen from their person in the same area but how and by whom they didn't know. They just found, when they wished to tell the time or they needed their money purse, that those articles were not in their pockets or where they should be. Mostly it was men who suffered. No one had reported seeing a young lady in difficulties anywhere and no one had reported finding one. Was his Buttercup lying dead somewhere or was she being subjected to other vile unpleasantness? It made him angry that he didn't know where to look or what to do.

Josh, however, had reached home and his mother gave a dose of medicine to Lavinia. It quietened her a little so Sal knew she had to be alert in three hours' time. There was a church nearby with a clock, which chimed the hour so she must remember to listen. Josh told his mother about the doctor mentioning Sir Nicholas. Did she think it a good idea if he, Josh, visited this person and told him about the girl? If he was pleased, there would be no trouble; if he was displeased, on the other hand, well, as his mother had said, Josh could move quickly and defend himself easily enough. The next thing, though, was to find where this Sir Nicholas lived.

'You've walked enough today, Josh,' said his mother. 'Your Pa will expect you in the boat this afternoon, you know, and it won't do for you to be tired.'

'Well, I've still a little money left so I'll take a cab if the driver knows where this fellow lives,' said Josh, 'and I can pay him enough.'

Josh had a drink, looked at Lavinia and shook his head. Then he was walking to the nearest place he knew of where the cabs waited for custom. The first driver he asked waved him away after looking at how he was dressed but the next driver wasn't so fussy. 'Do you know where Sir Nicholas Sinclair lives?' asked Josh.

'Oho, he's a friend of yours, is he?' he asked, with some sarcasm.

'No, of course not. But I have to see him,' said Josh.

'Right.' He shouted to a colleague. ''Ere mate, do you know where Sir Nicholas Sinclair lives?'

'Grosvenor Square—I've often delivered him back in the early morning very much the worse for wear,' was the answer.

'What number?'

'Dunno, but I wouldn't go if I were you.'

'I have to, I'm afraid,' said poor Josh, wondering what he had got himself into.

Josh had a chat about the price, which resulted in him handing over the rest of the money he had with the understanding that he would be set down at the end of Grosvenor Square. Then he would walk to whichever house he thought might be the right one.

It was a new experience for Josh to ride instead of walking everywhere, except when he was in his boat, of course, and in one way he was enjoying himself. He did hope something positive came of the trip but if not he would just have to work harder, if possible, to replace the money.

Grosvenor Square was quiet and a different world to the area near the river. Looking around he wondered which house he should try first. He picked one at random and knocked with the brass knocker on the door. It was opened by a superior being who looked down his nose. 'Tradesmen,' he began but Josh cut him short. 'Could you tell me where Sir Nicholas Sinclair lives, please?' he asked as nicely and carefully as he could.

The superior being nearly smiled thinking that it would be wonderful if he could see Sir Nicholas's face when confronted with this lowly person. So he said sharply, 'Number nine', and shut the door with a snap.

Josh didn't have time to thank him. Were all these kind of people rude, like that? If he was rude to his clients he'd never earn any money; besides, if he talked like that to people his parents would have something to say.

He knocked on the door of number nine and after a moment a bewigged lackey opened it.

'Could I see Sir Nicholas, please?' asked Josh. He found himself a little apprehensive, wondering what the man was like.

'I'm afraid...' began the lackey.

A voice from beyond asked: 'Who is it?'

'It is someone asking for Sir Nicholas, Mr Roberts.'

'Ask him in.'

The door was held open and Josh stepped into the grandest house he had ever been inside. He took off his hat and didn't move.

'Good morning, sir,' said Roberts, stepping forward. 'Can I help you in any way?'

'Could I see Sir Nicholas, please?'

'What is it about?'

'Well—a—a young lady.'

Roberts looked at him. He saw before him a tall, heavily built young man with an honest face. He was clean but his clothes proclaimed him of the working class.

He said: 'Please wait a moment, sir.'

Sir, thought Josh. Wait until he told his Ma!

Roberts came back. 'If you follow me, Sir Nicholas will see you now.'

So Josh, hat in hand, followed Roberts. 'Here is the gentleman, Sir Nicholas,' he announced.

Josh walked into the most beautiful room he had ever seen. Standing before him was a young man, good looking too if the worried look and frown were to be banished from his face.

'You wished to see me?' Sir Nicholas asked.

Josh, feeling a little uncomfortable in his working clothes, turned his hat in his hands. Then he remembered what he had rehearsed to say. 'Sir, my Father and I are ferrymen on the Thames and...'

He got no further. 'Oh, God, no,' said Sir Nicholas, turning away and rubbing his head.

'It's all right, sir. We were taking the boat home when we heard a splash. It was dark, you see, sir, and we shone the light and saw something in the water. It could have been just rubbish but we found this young lady. We took her to my Mother's and that is where she is now.'

'Who is it? Do you know?' Sir Nicholas asked eagerly.

'No, sir. You see, she is ill, not herself, but I went to the doctor to get her some medicine and she keeps mentioning your name sir.'

'Sit down, sit down,' said Sir Nicholas, walking backwards and forwards and rubbing his hand through his hair.

'But my clothes, sir,' said poor Josh, looking at the exquisite cushioned furniture.

Sir Nicholas just waved a hand at him.

'It is quite all right, sir, please sit down,' said Roberts.

'Now,' said Sir Nicholas, 'this girl calls my name. Anyone else?'

'She calls for her mother and Sophy, sir. Do you think you know her?'

'It sounds like the lady who is missing. Did you see who

did it?'

'No, sir. We just heard something. Many people dump rubbish in the river, sir.'

'But didn't you see anyone at all?' persisted Sir Nicholas.

'We were only concerned with what or who was in the water, sir. We vaguely noticed the shape of a boat but it was disappearing into the darkness,' said Josh, trying hard to explain that their concentration had been on a potential person drowning in the water.

'I see. Can I come and see her? To see if it is Miss Meadows as I expect?'

'Of course, sir. My mother's house is small but it is clean, sir, and she cooks well. The only thing is that my mother had to cut the lady's clothes off. They are dry now, I believe, but she won't be able to wear them and we have nothing decent to put on her. She has blankets round her now, sir.'

Sir Nicholas led Roberts to the door talking in a low voice. 'Order the carriage for me as soon as possible and if it is Miss Meadows I shall need a very large reward for these people. I should take blankets, I suppose.'

'A cloak, perhaps, would be easier, sir,' said Roberts.

'I shall take her to Lady Waverly as then I can be sure she will get the best medical attention possible. I'm not going to take her back to the Gilberts as they don't seem capable of looking after her at all.'

'No, sir, of course. I will arrange everything, don't worry.'

Twenty minutes later found Sir Nicholas in his carriage

with Josh sitting above with the driver as he had to tell him the way. Josh was enjoying himself as these people were relying on him and he just hoped that the girl his mother was looking after was the right one.

It didn't take long before they reached the river and the coachman carefully drove the pair of thoroughbreds down the crowded and narrow street. It stopped outside a little house near the river and Josh jumped down. As Sir Nicholas opened the door and looked round Josh asked him if he would wait until he had a word with his mother. Sir Nicholas nodded.

Josh knocked on the door and his mother opened it. 'Josh?' she said.

'I have brought Sir Nicholas to see if he knows the young lady. Is it all right for him to come inside?'

Josh's mother looked round, and seeing Sir Nicholas standing and waiting, dropped him a curtsey. 'Please come inside, sir. I have this moment lifted the young lady into a chair. She is still feverish but not as bad as she was.'

'Thank you,' said Sir Nicholas and followed Sal inside. His first thought was how clean and sweet smelling this tiny home was. He looked round eagerly and saw a small figure smothered in blankets, sitting in a large chair with her eyes closed. It was Lavinia. Sir Nicholas gave a deep sigh. 'Thank God, it is her,' he said. He went up to her and felt her forehead very gently. It was hot. He knelt down in front of her. 'Lavinia, look at me,' he said.

She seemed to know his voice as her eyelids flickered. He stroked her cheek. 'Come along, sweetheart, look at me.'

With a great effort she opened her eyes very briefly.

'Good girl,' Sir Nicholas said. 'I'm going to take you to Lady Waverly.' He turned to Sal. 'Could you possibly place my cloak around her instead of the blankets?'

'Yes, sir. I'll call Molly, Josh's wife. You had better take her clothes too, sir, but they're not much use, I'm afraid.'

'Throw them away. Lady Waverly will know what to do and Lavinia's mama will, I hope, be arriving shortly. Thank you so much for saving her life and looking after her so well.'

'We are pleased to do it, sir. My husband will be sorry to have missed you. He is working at the moment. Now sir, if you let me have the cloak and you stay outside for a moment, Josh will call his wife. Then when we are ready, perhaps you would carry this young lady out for me.'

It wasn't long before Lavinia was in Sir Nicholas's arms. He placed her inside the carriage as well as he could so that she lay on the seat. She groaned, apparently not feeling comfortable.

Sir Nicholas said his farewells to Sal, Molly and Josh, thanking them again for rescuing Lavinia. As he handed the bag of coins to Josh he said: 'If you are ever in trouble at any time, let me know.'

Josh just stood there saying 'thank you, sir,' while Sal and Molly curtseyed. Sir Nicholas climbed inside the coach and sat, holding Lavinia to him.

Josh, his wife and mother went indoors after the coach had disappeared from view and it was then that Josh let out a long whistle. 'Look!' he said. He had emptied the bag of coins onto the table. 'There's more money here than I've ever seen in my life.'

The two women looked on amazed. 'Good gracious,' said Sal, 'we must hide it.'

'And spend some of it,' laughed Molly.

CHAPTER
TWENTY TWO

THE COACH drew up outside the portico of Lady Waverly's large house and immediately the door was thrown open by two footmen who came out to help Sir Nicholas. As carefully as they could they lifted Lavinia from the coach and placed her in Sir Nicholas's arms. He entered the house to find the housekeeper standing and waiting.

'Follow me sir, if you please. Lady Waverly told us what to do and we are prepared for the young lady.'

Sir Nicholas followed the housekeeper up the stairs carrying Lavinia who moaned now and again. Eventually they reached the bedroom where a maid drew back the covers on the bed so that Sir Nicholas could lay Lavinia down.

'She has nothing on under this cloak, perhaps…'

'That is all right, sir,' interrupted the housekeeper. 'We will place her in one of Lady Waverly's nightgowns. Is this your cloak, sir?'

Sir Nicholas nodded.

'I will return it to you then. I'll place it in the hall where you can collect it when you leave, sir.'

'She is feverish and knows no one. She may be frightened,' began Sir Nicholas.

'That's all right, sir. We'll be very careful of her and I believe Lady Waverly has asked the doctor to call. We have placed a hot brick in the bed, too. So do you go downstairs to her ladyship now, sir, and we will make the young lady more comfortable.'

'Thank you,' said Sir Nicholas. 'You won't leave her, will you?'

'No sir, someone will stay with her at all times.'

Sir Nicholas nodded and much to the housekeeper's relief, left the room. Although later, she remarked, that a man in love must be pardoned for being so fussy about his young lady.

Sir Nicholas found Lady Waverly in her private sitting room. 'Come in, Nicholas and talk to me,' she smiled at him.

Sir Nicholas bowed and went over to kiss her cheek and then thankfully sank into a large comfortable chair. He looked round, thinking how much he liked this room with its soft colours and relaxed atmosphere.

Lady Waverly rang the bell and a servant entered with a tray of glasses and drinks. 'What would you like, Ma'am?' he asked.

'Nothing for me but I'm sure Sir Nicholas could do with a drink?' she smiled enquiringly at him.

'Brandy, please,' said Sir Nicholas, promptly.

When he was served and the servant had left the room, Lady Waverly looked at Sir Nicholas and saw how worried he was. 'Now tell me,' she said, 'what is this all about?'

He carefully explained what had happened. 'The people who looked after her were very kind. I suppose she was lucky that they found her. But until I know what happened I can't do anything, can I?'

'Certainly not,' said Lady Waverly. 'You did exactly right. Have you any idea why she was found in the Thames? She couldn't have been suicidal, surely?'

'I'm sure she wasn't. No, someone did the foul deed and someone is going to pay for it,' said Sir Nicholas.

'Mm, yes,' said Lady Waverly slowly, looking at Sir Nicholas's dark face. 'But don't be in too much of a hurry to apportion blame. First, we must wait for Lavinia to recover, then she will probably tell us what happened.'

'And let us hope that will be soon,' said Sir Nicholas. 'I must go. Thank you for having her. I will write a note to the Gilberts as they are worried. Also, I will ask them to send the rest of Lavinia's clothes here, if that is all right?'

'Yes, of course. Perhaps you could mention she is not seeing visitors at the moment, as she is not fully recovered? And Nicholas, don't rush Lavinia into marriage. Go carefully with her.'

Sir Nicholas nodded then went to kiss Lady Waverly's cheek. 'Thank you as always for your help.' He turned as he opened the door. 'You will let me know as soon as she is well enough to see me?'

'Of course,' smiled Lady Waverly reassuringly.

Sir Nicholas saw Roberts as soon as he entered the house.

'Any news, sir?' Roberts asked.

Sir Nicholas smiled. 'Thank you, yes. The ferryman had

rescued Miss Meadows but she was feverish and didn't know me. I took her to Lady Waverly's and everyone was ready to receive her. She will be well looked after, I know, and I shall be told as soon as Miss Meadows recovers. Then I can visit. Meanwhile I must write two letters. One to Miss Meadows' parents, which must go by courier. Could that be arranged? The other I must write to the Gilberts and perhaps whoever you send can take Miss Meadows's clothes to Lady Waverly? If you can arrange everything, I will write now.'

Sir Nicholas entered his study and sat down at the beautiful old desk that had belonged to his father. He drew out a sheet of headed notepaper and began to write.

After Sir Nicholas had sprinkled sand on the letters and addressed them he went to the door where Roberts was waiting for them. He ordered the carriage to be brought round to take him to Bow Street where he told them that Miss Meadows had been found and was recovering at Lady Waverly's but on no account were they to visit. They were pleased to know this but as yet they had no idea who was behind the abduction or the thefts.

At last, Sir Nicholas, pleased to think that he had done all he could at the moment, sat down to enjoy a glass of wine in his library, which Roberts had so thoughtfully brought for him.

Two days later Lavinia began to stir. She had just laid in bed at Lady Waverly's, asleep and murmuring words that no one could understand. She had had someone watching over her at all times but no one as yet had any news of any improvement. The doctor had called every day and was confident that all would be well eventually and now she was beginning to open her eyes.

She expected to be in the dark but it was daylight. Her throat felt uncomfortable and dry; she needed a drink. She tried to ask but no voice came so she began to cry. Then the door opened and a young girl came in with a jug.

'Oh, Miss,' she said, 'you're awake. Would you like a drink? I'll call Rachel to help you.' She went to the door and called while Lavinia stopped crying at the magic word 'drink.'

Rachel came in. 'Oh my dear Miss Meadows, you are awake. Thank goodness. Now let us raise you up and you can have some of this fresh lemon and barley water.'

Lavinia thought she had never tasted anything so good. Afterwards she managed to ask where she was.

'This is Lord and Lady Waverly's house. I shall tell her now that you have woken up. There is no need to worry, Miss.'

Lavinia managed to smile and murmur 'thank you' before she went back to sleep once more.

The next time she awoke Lady Waverly was sitting with her. 'Oh, my dear,' she said. 'How are you feeling?'

'I—I'm all right, I think. Why am I here?' Then all the evils she had been through began to come into her mind. 'It was awful and I couldn't do anything. The coalhouse was the worst and it was so cold. Oh, oh, and the river! I went into the river, I remember. What happened? Those men were evil.' She buried her face in her hands.

'It is all right now, Lavinia,' murmured Lady Waverly. 'I

am here. You are quite safe.'

'Yes, yes, but where is Sir Nicholas?'

'He will be here as soon as you are able to rise from your bed. Would you like something to eat, dear?'

'No, no, just a drink. Thank you.' She drank more of the barley water and slept once more.

It was three days later when Lady Waverly sent a message to Sir Nicholas saying that Miss Meadows was much improved and had been asking to see him. Sir Nicholas smiled and let out a sigh of relief. First and foremost, he was pleased his love was herself again, but he had been waiting impatiently to hear her part of the story and who was involved in it.

As usual he dressed with care and first visited the florist to buy two bouquets of flowers, one for each of the ladies. In both cases he chose a mixture of white and pink roses. A servant at Lady Waverly's house said he would take Sir Nicholas to the ladies who were in the garden room. Sir Nicholas knew this room and he was delighted to think that Lavinia was well enough to sit there as he had wondered if she had been allowed by the doctor to leave her bedchamber at all.

The room was prettily decorated in shades of pink with cream and pink rugs and pictures on the walls of flowers and romantic figures. It overlooked a flower garden, which also had flowering bushes and a willow tree.

The servant announced Sir Nicholas and Lady Waverly went forward to greet him. 'Nicholas, come and see our invalid, don't you think she is looking well? Oh, and you have brought us some flowers! How nice of you. That will cheer us both. Thank you.' She took her bouquet, sniffing the perfume of the roses.

Sir Nicholas immediately strode over to Lavinia. She had stood up when he had arrived and he noticed how pale and tired she looked. He took her hand and kissed it. 'Sit down, my love. We have a lot to talk about, haven't we?'

'Yes, yes,' said Lavinia, thankful to sit down again as her knees seemed to be made of water.

'I will leave you then,' said Lady Waverly. 'I'll tell the servant to bring in your arrangement of flowers, Lavinia,' she said, taking both bouquets of roses. 'They are so pretty.'

Sir Nicholas opened the door for Lady Waverly and then returned to sit by Lavinia. 'Are you comfortable here?' he asked.

She nodded.

'I think it would be better if I placed my arm around you though, and then you can lean on me. These couches are pretty to look at but are sometimes damned uncomfortable.'

Lavinia didn't mind having Sir Nicholas's strong arm around her. She even smiled. She felt safe and secure and, as he probably had guessed, it was easier for her to talk to him without looking at him. So with her head now on his shoulder he began.

'I think, if you can manage it, my love, you had better tell me how you came to be missing when you went walking with your friend and then I shall be able to tell you what happened next.'

'Sir Nicholas, do you know why Mama isn't here? Do

my family know...?'

He interrupted. 'Yes, they do know. I sent a letter to them to say you were being taken care of by Lady Waverly and when you are well enough I will take you home. There is no need for you to worry. I visited them previously to ask your Papa for your hand in marriage, you know, and they will be pleased to have you home for a while.'

'Did Papa give his permission?' asked Lavinia.

'Of course, and your Mama was pleased, too. So tell me what you can remember, my love, and then I'll tell you what I know.'

'I went to stay with Sophy and her family. It was fun. One day we went to this street which was quite pretty with its shops and...and...' Her voice broke. She swallowed hard and then continued. 'Some friends of Sophy's saw us and came over and I was introduced but I didn't know them and they talked about things I didn't know about. I didn't mind, of course, and I just stood with them and then I saw someone I knew on the other side of the road.'

Sir Nicholas felt Lavinia shaking. He tightened his arm around her. 'Who was it, my love?'

'It—it was M de Craon and he was with another man. M de Craon was chatting to people and being quite pleasant but the other man took their purses and things from their pockets without them knowing. I—I was horrified. If only I hadn't stared at them. But I was so shocked. If I'd been quicker I could have looked in a window or something but...'

'But? Go on, love.'

'M de Craon saw me staring and they both came over

to me and stood either side of me. And do you know,' Lavinia said looking up at Sir Nicholas, 'he spoke perfect English? I mean he had no accent.'

Sir Nicholas kissed her. 'Did he now? Go on, my love.'

'The other man didn't say a word. In fact, he never spoke at any time. Do you think he wasn't able to?'

'Possibly. Go on.'

'Well, M de Craon said he would show me some jewellery in a side window and it was in an alleyway. I had to go as one of them was either side of me and they manoeuvred me apart from the others. I tried to struggle but they snatched me and they led me to the back of the buildings where there were coal houses with bars across the doors. They opened one and pushed me inside. I heard them place the bar across and I was left. It was dark and damp but empty. I tried to feel around the walls but they were just damp. I tried shouting but my voice wasn't strong enough and no one heard me. And I remember crying as no one knew where I was and—and I needed you so badly. In the finish I sat down and tucked my skirts around me and hugged myself. It—it was so cold. When they came for me it was dark and I was frozen. M de Craon threw a smelly blanket over me and picked me up. Neither of them spoke. I was carried down the street, I suppose, and I was then laid on something. I think it was a cart as I was bumped over the cobbles and I could hear the horse's hooves. After a short while it stopped and I was lifted up and the next thing I saw was the river. I was thrown in a boat and held down until—until—I—I—was tipped out. I tried to shout but my mouth filled with water and I—I don't remember anything else. It was horrid.' She clung tightly to Sir Nicholas. She was trembling.

'Poor sweetheart,' he said. 'Tell me, did they do anything else to you that they shouldn't have done?'

'No. It—it was just as I said.'

'Well, I can tell you,' said Sir Nicholas, 'that you were very lucky as you were picked up by the ferrymen. Josh and his father took you home and got you breathing again. Their wives looked after you. They tried to feed you but you became feverish and Josh was so concerned he went to a doctor and paid for some medicine for you. It must have been a lot of money for him. Evidently, you called for your Mama, Sophy—and me. And Josh cleverly found out where I lived and came to see me. He was uncomfortable as he thought he was too dirty to sit on my furniture, I remember. We went back to his parents' house and I went in to see if it was really you and thank goodness, my darling, it was.' He hugged her tighter. 'I brought you back to Lady Waverly. I also let your family know, as I have said, and I also let the Gilberts know and asked them not to visit you until you were well again. But I did ask them to let you have your clothes.'

'Oh, thank you. I should like to see them again and to explain a little, and those people who rescued me—I must repay them for their help and kindness. Oh, Sir Nicholas,' she gasped, 'I nearly died.'

'Yes, my love, I know, but you didn't and I repaid Josh for you. Also, I think you can stop calling me 'Sir,' don't you, as we're going to be married?'

'Oh, oh, are we?' she asked breathlessly. She realised this was just what she wanted and what she had hoped for a long time now. Sir Nicholas didn't frighten her anymore.

'You don't think that I went all the way to Kent to ask your Papa for his permission, which he gave, and then not marry you? I went to the Gilberts too and you weren't there and now I have found you, you are going to say yes, aren't you?'

There was a timid knock on the door.

'Who the devil is that?' said Sir Nicholas, getting up and opening the door.

A servant stood there with a decanter of sherry and two glasses on a silver tray. 'Lady Waverly sent this, sir…' began the man.

'Yes, thank you,' said Sir Nicholas, impatiently taking the tray and placing it on a table.

The door shut once more and Sir Nicholas repeated his question.

'But—but I thought you might have changed your mind.'

'No,' said Sir Nicholas and placed both arms round her, fastened his lips to hers and kissed her until she struggled for breath. 'Do you still think I might have changed my mind?' he asked.

'No—no,' was all she could manage before she was ruthlessly kissed again.

Someone knocked on the door. 'Not again! Who is it this time?' said Sir Nicholas, looking annoyed but getting up to open it.

It was only a servant holding a vase of the beautiful roses Sir Nicholas had brought. 'Thank you,' he said, taking it.

The door shut and the vase was placed on a small table near Lavinia. 'Oh, how lovely they are. Thank you,' she said.

'Now are you going to marry me or not?' asked her nearly demented suitor.

'Oh yes, I so love roses,' she said with a mischievous smile.

CHAPTER
TWENTY THREE

'**AND MAY I ASK** if your mission prospered, sir?' enquired Roberts as he took Sir Nicholas's coat and hat.

Sir Nicholas grinned at him. 'Thank you, Roberts, it did indeed. Come in and drink a toast to my future wife and me.'

'With pleasure, sir. May I tell the butler first? They are all agog below stairs and hope for a little celebration.'

'Of course.' Sir Nicholas felt he had a right to be pleased with himself. His love was safe and well on the way to recovery from her ordeal—and what an ordeal it had been for one so young and innocent. He must plan something to right that wrong and tomorrow he would put this plan into action.

Roberts came back bringing a tray of drinks and verbal congratulations, he said, from the butler on behalf of all the staff who were celebrating with a drink.

Sir Nicholas grinned. 'There will be more to celebrate later. I shall have to arrange something to include everyone but I don't want to put too much pressure on Miss Meadows too soon.'

'Perhaps her mother could help you there, sir,' said Roberts.

'Yes, of course, or Lady Waverly, perhaps. Meanwhile,' went on Sir Nicholas, pointing to a chair for Roberts to sit on while he took the one opposite, 'meanwhile there is a small task of M de Craon, whoever he really is.'

'Why, sir?'

'Well, I can't leave him at large, can I? He is a danger to Miss Meadows. She knows too much about him. If he knew she was still alive, his one aim, I should imagine, would be to kill her. Roberts, she isn't safe. He'll have to be disposed of. Also Bow Street are looking for him and his accomplice but I can't rely on them for Miss Meadows' safety.'

'I see the problem, sir,' said Roberts, looking worried. 'But you will be careful? We don't want Miss Meadows to die of a broken heart, do we?'

Sir Nicholas smiled. 'No, but I shouldn't think it will come to that. I think the sooner the deed is done the better.'

'Can I go with you, sir? I wouldn't get in your way but...'

'No, no. You're a dear friend and always have been, but this I must do alone.'

Roberts bowed, thanked him for the drink and left Sir Nicholas to his plans.

The following morning Sir Nicholas was up bright and early. He breakfasted as usual and no one looking at him could tell of his intentions. He was dressed in subdued clothes of black with silver trim but by no means did he look anything less than a well dressed young man. One thing he did spend his time on was the cleaning and polishing of his sword. He usually checked every morning to see that it was sharp and as clean as possible. One didn't know when it would be needed, as there were some desperate and dangerous villains around.

By mid-morning he was ready to leave. 'Please come back safely, sir,' said Roberts as he closed the carriage door on Sir Nicholas, who just grinned and said: 'Of course.'

He was taken as far as possible in Hammersmith and when he climbed out of the carriage there were only a few steps before he entered the street at the same place as Lavinia and Sophy had done previously. Sir Nicholas was impressed by the amount of people walking there and gradually he joined the shoppers, looking in windows and generally getting to know the layout of the area. He soon located the shop that sold jewellery and although he only glanced briefly in the window he realised the quality of the contents. He noticed the alleyway at the side of the shop and casually strolled down until he came to the place where Lavinia was imprisoned. He was determined more than ever to end de Craon's life. Although he was angry inside he was deadly calm outside and retraced his steps to where there was laughter from the ladies and gentlemen meeting friends and enjoying the beautiful goods in the shop windows. He noticed the art shop with its pictures and it was while he was glancing in the window that it reflected a figure he knew. It was the gentleman from Bow Street. So he was after M de Craon as well, was he? Now would he be a help or a hindrance? At the moment, of course, their prey didn't seem to be present but Sir Nicholas decided to keep away from the Bow Street gentleman otherwise things might be difficult. So he walked along slowly, looking in shop windows, pretending to be someone who was enjoying a pleasant morning.

Then he saw them, M de Craon and his partner. They blended in well with the crowd and no one would suspect them of anything untoward. Now where was the man from Bow Street? Sir Nicholas couldn't see him. Perhaps he was in a doorway. As he watched, M de Craon and his partner began. He bumped into a gentleman and as he was giving him his prolonged apologies his partner quickly relieved the victim of his purse. It was so quickly done, it really was clever, thought Sir Nicholas. He couldn't help but admire the dexterity of the man. Then it happened again. Sir Nicholas crossed the road, being careful to keep himself with other people so he wouldn't be noticed. He saw a turning, which led to the back of the shops and he went down it a little way. This would do nicely, he thought. He slowly made his way back to the main street again but stopped at the corner and waited. M de Craon and his accomplice were walking slowly along, one chatting, one pointing out things in the various windows. In between doing this, they robbed any likely wealthy gentlemen.

At last Sir Nicholas's patience in waiting for the two men to come abreast of him paid off. He stepped forward in front of them. 'Good morning, gentlemen, I trust you are having a profitable morning?' he said

M de Craon stood still and Sir Nicholas saw him lose colour. 'I—I do not...' he began.

'Perhaps you and your friend will give me a moment of your time?' Sir Nicholas by this time had swiftly drawn his sword and was now gently herding them into the alleyway away from the crowd.

'But why the sword? I am quite happy to speak to you. My friend, I'm afraid, cannot.'

'So who are you really? No Frenchman.'

'Er—well—no. But that is a long story.'

'I'm sure it is. So instead of stealthily bringing out your sword and hoping your friend is doing the same, let me tell you I'm going to kill you for treating Miss Meadows so badly. She told me the whole.'

'She can't have done so. I mean...'

'Oh, yes. There are ferrymen on the Thames, my friend, and they rescued her.' And with these words Sir Nicholas began the attack. As usual his strokes were quick and at the same time he kept a wary eye on the other man who tried to edge round Sir Nicholas so that they had him between them. But Sir Nicholas was in his element and he was nimble and quick and although the others knew how to use a sword they were no match for him. He drove them deeper into the alleyway, and away from the street.

Sir Nicholas was ruthless. He now had them both in front of him but he concentrated on the Frenchman. He sliced through his opponent's wrist. 'That is for leaving Miss Meadows in the dark,' he said.

They began to hit out more wildly and although de Craon's friend did his best he was no match for the quickness of Sir Nicholas's sword. He now plunged it into

M de Craon's shoulder. 'That is for frightening Miss Meadows,' he said, deadly calm. They wouldn't hold out much longer and he began to think he must make an end. Which one first? His eyes darted from one to the other, the sweat running into his eyes. 'And this is for nearly drowning her.' He quickly struck M de Craon through the heart.

When de Craon's friend saw what had happened he quickly turned and ran off as fast as he could.

Sir Nicholas had done what he came to do. He sheathed his sword and without a backwards glance at the body on the ground walked away. Now he could sleep quiet in his bed at night. His love was safe.

Next day Sir Nicholas decided to visit his beloved in the afternoon and left Grosvenor Square taking with him a slim parcel. He found Lord and Lady Waverly sitting in the withdrawing room with Lavinia, taking tea. This was a very elegant room in soft blues and creams. The roses Sir Nicholas had taken previously were standing on a small delicate table near to where Lady Waverly was sitting.

'Come in, dear boy,' said Lord Waverly. 'Can it be you have come to take tea with us?' He said this with a cheeky grin on his face.

Sir Nicholas smiled. 'Thank you, no, sir. Ma'am,' he said as he bowed over Lady Waverly's hand.

'I don't suppose he wishes to see us at all,' laughed Lady Waverly. 'So come along, my dear, we will leave these two to chat.'

Her husband laughed.

CHAPTER TWENTY THREE

Sir Nicholas turned to a blushing Lavinia. 'And how are you today?'

Lavinia had risen and curtsied. 'I am much better, sir, I thank you.'

'Good,' he said sitting down beside her. He put his hand in his pocket and brought out a slender box. 'This is for you, my love.'

'A present? Gracious, how nice. What is it, I wonder?' She opened the box very carefully to find the most beautiful fan imaginable lying there. 'Oh, how wonderful! Is it really for me?'

'It is, my love. It was my Mama's and I thought you might like to have it.'

Most of the fans Lavinia had seen were brightly coloured and decorated with classical scenes from myths or legends but this one was of delicate white lace mounted on ivory sticks with vignettes of coloured wild flowers. It looked very expensive and very, very pretty.

'It is so beautiful, thank you,' Lavinia said, admiring it and not wanting to put it down. 'I wish I had something to give you,' she smiled.

'You have given me all that I want which is to marry you, my darling,' laughed Sir Nicholas, kissing her.

CHAPTER
TWENTY FOUR

MISS DRUSILLA SONNING descended from her carriage with an effort. She had come from her home which was only two streets away but that was much too far for her to walk. Now she slowly climbed the steps to the front door and let fall the knocker. The door opened.

'Oh, Miss Sonning, how nice to see you,' said the doorman.

'May I see Miss Kelloe?'

By this time the housekeeper had arrived. 'Oh, good morning, Miss Sonning, do come in.'

'How is my friend? May I see her?'

'Miss Kelloe is still not herself, Miss, but if you would like to go up I'm sure she would be pleased to see you. I was just taking her these letters. Not that she opens them,' she finished with a sigh.

'Let me take them to her,' said Dru. She quickly looked through them. There were two bills, she was sure, and an envelope like the one she herself had brought. Dru smiled.

It was a full fifteen minutes later, for she had to climb the stairs, that she was knocking on Effie's door.

'Come in,' said a frail voice from the other side.

CHAPTER TWENTY FOUR

'Good morning, Effie, my dear. How do you find yourself this morning?'

'Oh, hello, dear. Not good, not good,' Effie replied, looking mournful.

'Here are your letters, dear, and you should…'

'I don't want them. They're always the same, bills and bills. Do sit down, Dru, and tell me what brings you here.'

'Have you had any breakfast at all, dear?' asked Dru as she carefully sat on an armchair.

'Only a little. Just tea and toast,' said Effie sadly.

By the look of her plate and the crusts she had left she had consumed quite a lot of toast.

'Why are you so down, my dear?' asked Dru.

'Nobody wants us, Dru. There are no invitations, there's nothing to look forward to.'

'But, my dear, invitations are in short supply this time of year. When the season starts again I'm sure we shall be needed, you know.'

'But we weren't invited to Sir Nicholas's wedding and I thought we should have been,' lamented poor Effie.

'Oh, I see,' said Dru, 'so that's at the bottom of it all, is it? Now Effie, you know very well they had a quiet wedding in Kent as the poor little bride had had a terrible time at the hands of that—that Frenchman fellow. I expect Sir Nicholas wanted her to be quite well before they celebrated in a lavish way. They had a quiet wedding and afterwards travelled to Sinclair House for a little while for the new Lady Sinclair to recover. I believe when she was better they went to Paris for a while,' finished Dru enviously.

'I quite see that the poor little thing would have been terrified by what had happened to her, but I so wanted to be at the wedding,' said Effie, dabbing her eyes.

'I expect a lot of people did. Lord and Lady Waverly attended, of course, and they said it was a pretty wedding at the village church and the bride's dress was in pale pink decorated with white embroidery. She would have looked quite sweet, wouldn't she?'

Effie nodded, still dabbing at her eyes.

'Also,' went on Dru, 'Lord and Lady Waverly are to hold a special ball for them in a few weeks time for all their friends to attend.'

'Really? How do you know?' asked poor Effie with a sniff.

'Because I have had an invitation,' said Dru, waving the card triumphantly in the air.

'Do you think I shall have one?' asked a pathetic Effie.

'If you only opened your letters, dear, you might find out.' And she passed over the special envelope she had carried up the stairs.

On reading it Effie's face was wreathed in smiles. 'Oh, I have an invitation too! Oh, Dru, isn't it wonderful?' Her face, so melancholy before, was now alight with pleasure. 'Oh, Dru, Dru, do you think we should go shopping? We shall need dresses and...'

'Oh, yes,' said Dru, 'we must definitely go shopping. We must buy presents, you know, and what do you think we should wear? And we must have new shoes, comfortable ones and...'

Effie, now a different woman and beaming all over her face, said she thought she could eat some breakfast after all and Dru was welcome to join her, after which they would feel fit enough to venture out to buy a lovely gift for Sir Nicholas and his bride. They would also visit the shops for new dresses, which would be fun as neither of them had a rag to their backs, they said, and then perhaps they could treat themselves to one of those new flavoured ices?